MW01611545

FIGHTING FOR MARCY (POLICE AND FIRE: OPERATION ALPHA

BADGE OF HONOR: TARPLEY VFD, SEASON 2 #2

MJ NIGHTINGALE

This book is a work of fiction. Names, characters, places, and incidents are products of the author's imagination or used fictitiously. Any resemblance to actual events or locales or persons living or dead is entirely coincidental.

© 2020 ACES PRESS, LLC. ALL RIGHTS RESERVED

No part of this work may be used, stored, reproduced or transmitted without written permission from the publisher except for brief quotations for review purposes as permitted by law. This book is licensed for your personal enjoyment only. This book may not be re-sold or given away to other people. If you would like to share this book with another person, please purchase an additional copy for each recipient. If you're reading this book and did not purchase it, or it was not purchased for your use only, please purchase your own copy.

Editing: Goller Editing

Cover Design: © Buoni Amici Press, LLC

Dear Readers,

Welcome to the Police and Fire: Operation Alpha Fan-Fiction world!

If you are new to this amazing world, in a nutshell the author wrote a story using one or more of my characters in it. Sometimes that character has a major role in the story, and other times they are only mentioned briefly. This is perfectly legal and allowable because they are going through Aces Press to publish the story.

This book is entirely the work of the author who wrote it. While I might have assisted with brainstorming and other ideas about which of my characters to use, I didn't have any part in the process or writing or editing the story.

I'm proud and excited that so many authors loved my characters enough that they wanted to write them into their own story. Thank you for supporting them, and me!

READ ON!
    Xoxo
    Susan Stoker

To our wonderful readers: This second set of Tarpley Volunteer Fire Department books have been as much fun to write as the originals. The TVFD family is expanding with new volunteers—heroes and heroines —and the ones they're meant to be with. Five talented authors with different styles and ideas creating a series can be a challenge but brainstorming how all our characters could interact was far more fun than a chore. It's amazing what the folks in one small Texas town and the surrounding county can get up to. Each story stands alone with a HEA and no cliffhanger at the end, though we share the world and characters do cross over into other books. That's part of the fun—for us as authors and hopefully for all of you as readers. We hope you'll enjoy the individual styles. Not all details may match because the stories are told from various points of view. Our goal is to entertain you and offer an opportunity to leave the real world behind and get lost in the lives and loves of our characters. Thank you for your support and happy reading!

~TL, MJ, Haven, Deanndra, and Silver

TABLE OF CONTENTS

"You need to take this call, Blake," the sheriff stated, popping his head out of his office. Jack Riggs was his new boss. He was the epitome of a Texas county sheriff. Tall, lean, looked like Sam Elliot, only younger. His face always had that grim expression of impending doom. At least while on the job. And he took his job seriously. Always. He wasn't a bullshitter and dealt with people straight. "Line 2, Deputy." Riggs went back to his office, leaving the door open. He always left his door open.

Blake liked him. It made the transfer from his previous post easier to swallow. Blake had not gotten along with his former sergeant in New York and needed a change of scenery after what had happened between him and his former co-workers. He was all for the blue line. But he would not tolerate dirty cops or look the other way.

He had needed the slower pace, too. An early marriage in his twenties had soured him on commitment. The divorce within a year of the wedding ceremony taught him a lesson he had not soon forgotten. His wife had cheated on him and asked for a divorce. She ended up marrying a bar owner in Jersey a few years later. He'd let her go. He didn't even hold a grudge. Not anymore.

When he saw an online posting for a deputy with investigative experience from a small county in Texas, he gave it a shot. The sheriff wanted someone with detective experience to handle a backlog of cold cases and any new murder cases that may crop up.

Sheriff Jack Riggs called him the next day and he had flown in for an interview. Riggs offered him the job on the spot. The man he replaced had moved to Houston looking for more adventure. Blake accepted the position. He wasn't leaving too much behind in New York and his folks had retired to Arizona years earlier.

"Serious?" Blake asked, pushing aside the pile of cold cases the sheriff had given him to look into on Monday. It was Friday. They hadn't had any major crimes reported all week. This would be his first live case.

"Yup," Riggs hollered back across the room. It was a small office. Five desks and three other deputies who handled drug cases, theft, vandalism, sex crimes and other lesser crimes and did their patrols. But Riggs had wanted to fill the vacancy with someone who specialized in murder. And he had plenty of experience there. In ten years as detective, he closed over 275 cases. He only failed to close three. Good numbers. Riggs had been impressed.

Not that Banderas had a lot of murder, thankfully. There had been only nineteen in the past five years. But the cold cases were pretty high. Lots of bodies in the desert, mostly illegals crossing the border, but still, they needed to be reviewed each year and crosschecked with missing person's cases. He had also been given some of those. Mostly young girls. Another deputy had a pile twice as high as his. He would be busy, though he wouldn't be handed a new murder case each week like he had been when he was in New York.

Blake picked up the receiver on the old phone he'd been given and hit line two. "Deputy Blake Levine speaking. How can I help you?"

"Yeah, man, hey, it's, James, from The Depot up in Tarpley. One of my waitresses overheard a conversation last night. Just told me about it today. Not sure if it's anything, but I thought I'd let Riggs know, just in case." The Depot was a watering hole in Tarpley that had become the go-to hangout since Randy's had been flattened by a tornado a few months back, he'd been told. It boasted live music and was a popular hangout for the Tarpley Volunteer Fire Department members.

He'd get the guy's last name later. "Sure, James. What'd she overhear?" Blake asked, wondering where this was going. Didn't sound like someone was dead. The man's voice was pretty calm.

"My girl, Susie, one of my waitresses, she heard some blonde drunk girl talking to one of our local bikers. A guy they call Snake. She was sniffing around him for a while and asked him if he would kill someone for her if the price was right." Blake's interest was piqued now. But the girl, the blonde, was drunk. So there was that, but Riggs wanted him to look into it and take this threat seriously. He was glad he had the time. "Snake told her to fuck off," James added.

"Good for Snake," Blake commented. It could be nothing, Blake thought, but he'd go and talk to the waitress, maybe the biker, too. His first road trip. He'd be glad to get out of the office and stretch his legs. "Is Susie working today?"

"Yeah, she's here now. Just told me about it. She works until closing at two."

Blake glanced at the clock on the wall of the large room. It was four in the afternoon. He had been clocking out around five each day but had nothing else to do tonight. "I'll be there in an hour." Blake hung up and made his way over to Jack's office after closing his files and locking them in his desk drawer.

"I'm going to check this one out, Sergeant." Blake slipped and went to correct himself, but Jack held up his hand. He was getting used to the new titles in his current position and had slipped a couple of times, mistakenly calling the sheriff "Sarge."

"You'll figure it out, New York. Yes, go. Good idea. Keep me posted. And since you're going to Tarpley, might as well drop off your paperwork to Pops at the fire station."

"What paperwork?"

One of the first things Riggs had done upon hiring him was to convince him to join the Volunteer Fire

Department in Tarpley. "Folks around here? They look at you and see big city. You need to think about joining Tarpley's volunteer fire department. That'll get you some contacts. And as folks get used to you, they'll open up." Blake recalled his words after he offered him the job.

Blake had liked the idea but hadn't gotten round to it yet. He wasn't terribly surprised when Riggs pulled the paperwork out of his desk. He laughed. "You just happen to have the paperwork, Riggs."

"Pops and I go way back. He knew my new hire would want to join the crew and gave it to me last week. Thought you might go out there on your own, but gave it to me just in case."

"I only just moved. I'm still settling in."

"Just cause it's Texas, and the South, don't mean we handle shit slow. We take care of business."

"Yes, sir." Blake got the message.

"It's Riggs, Jack, or Sheriff. No 'sir' stuff here."

"Got it, Jack."

CHAPTER 2

"That's Susie over there." James pointed at the cute waitress carrying a tray of beers that looked heavier than she weighed. "I'll call her over."

Blake turned back toward the bar. He was done with cute waitresses. He'd had his share. Another reason why he'd left New York. People were too restless in the city, and no one seemed ready to settle down. He was nearing forty, and though he looked much younger and was in tip-top shape health- wise, he wanted a family. Tired of being alone, he was ready to try again.

He gazed at his reflection in the mirror behind the bottles of expensive liquor, along with local brands. His hair was still a thick wavy black, and his face held a bit of stubble from his shave this morning with small lines on the brow and around the eyes. He'd find her, he vowed. A woman he could spend his life loving. He wanted a family and Texas was where he planned to start it.

He decided on a Coke, and James went to fill his glass while he waited for Susie to approach. He had gone home to change before heading out. He had taken off the jacket and tie he wore when canvassing neighborhoods. The suit worked fine when you were talking to people in the suburbs, but in a bar in Texas it was better to fit in with the local crowd. He had worn a simple western shirt and a pair of jeans and sneakers. He wasn't ready to break in boots just yet.

"Hi, I'm Susie." The girl approached from the side. "You're the deputy, James said." The girl sounded breathless.

"Yes, um, Deputy Levine. Blake." He was getting used to the new title and informality of Texas.

"I don't know how much more I can tell you. The girl was in her mid-twenties, blonde, pretty, and she was wearing a neon green tank top showing off her assets for anyone to see. I don't recall her shorts or anything."

"How long had she been in the bar, do you know?" he asked.

"Hmm, quite some time. She was drunk, or appeared to be. She was flirting with Snake something fierce. Leaning on him. Buying her own drinks, though. Snake has an old lady so he knows better, but he didn't seem to mind the attention."

"What's awhile?" Blake asked for clarification on the timeline.

"I guess about two hours. Came in around eleven and left after Snake told her to fuck off. I was picking up a few pitchers and bottles from James right next to

7

her. That's why I heard what was said. She leaned in all close and flirtatious like and whispered in his ear, but I heard every word. She said, 'Hey Snake, would you kill a person for me if the price was right?' He blew up at her. He is MC, but he ain't a bad man. He told her to fuck off. She was embarrassed and turned on her heel and left the bar right after that."

"No one left after her that you know of?"

Susie shook her head. "No, Deputy. Snake just started laughing after that and talking to some of the other guys he came in with then."

"And where can I find this Snake guy?"

"Hmm, well you are going to have ask James, or maybe José, the manager. I am not sure where he lives or what his real name is, but they might know. The club members have a running tab here, so I'm sure one of them must know."

"Thanks, Susie. If you think of anything else call me." He gave her his card and she slipped it into the front of her apron pocket.

James came over when Susie went back to work. From James he learned the place had no cameras. They hadn't been replaced yet since the tornado came flying though. And James promised he would get back to him with a name. The MC were funny that way, and he couldn't go around giving names without asking for permission first. "I will have Snake call you. He's a decent guy, but I don't want to mess with the MC if I don't have to."

"Fair enough," Blake conceded. "Here's my card. Have him call this number."

"Will do, Deputy."

"Thanks, James." Blake dropped a ten on the counter and walked out without his change.

When Blake left The Depot, he saw a Rite-Aid down the block and thought he'd try his luck there for cameras. However, the Rite-Aid was in the same situation as The Depot. Apparently, security cameras were not a priority at the moment.

Blake hopped into his vehicle as his cell phone rang. "Levine," he answered.

"You the cop?" a man growled into the phone.

"Yes, this Snake?" Blake guessed.

"Yes, and it's Matthew Foreman. Sorry about James not giving you my name. But we have a policy."

"Got it."

"I understand you wanted to know about last night. Girl was hitting on me, grabbing my crotch. It happens. Some girls see an MC and like to take ride on the wild side. I'm game with that, but we got rules. My old lady was at The Depot with her gal pals, eyeballing me across the bar. I can look but not touch, so I let the blonde think she was getting somewhere. For fun. Anyhow, she flipped on a dime and asked me to kill a guy, and I told her to fuck off. That's pretty much it. She had on a green shirt. Didn't see nothin' else because I was just looking at her tits."

"She wanted you to off a guy?" Blake asked.

"Actually, she didn't say. She said kill a person," Snake corrected. That jived with what the waitress had said. So now he was no closer to the would-be hire-for-murder person or the victim. Just great.

Blake knew the man was being honest. "Thanks for calling me, Snake, and if you think of anything else, at all, even the smallest detail, give me a holler. I don't want this woman finding someone else to do her dirty work without knowing who she is or who she is after."

"Got you." Snake hung up without another word.

Blake almost called it a night, but then saw the fire station and decided now was as good a time as any to take care of the packet of paperwork sitting beside him in the vehicle. He made a quick turn and pulled up next to several cars already parked there.

It was time he joined his own club.

CHAPTER 3

Marsha had lunch with her friend Jemma in the break-room at Medina High School. They had both come in early to set up their classrooms before the rush in two weeks when all the faculty arrived back from their summer vacations. Jemma herself had just gotten back from a quick honeymoon in Florida.

"You look amazing. I guess your honeymoon agreed with you," Marsha teased her friend.

"It did." Jemma blushed. She had enjoyed the week vacation in Florida where she had gotten to meet her cousin Bella Marino, her only living relative. Her cousin's husband's family, a rowdy group of former New York police officers turned bounty hunters, had welcomed her and Angel with open arms. The four brothers were tight, as were their wives. Jemma was glad Bella had an extended family, like she did with Angel and the TVFD. Bella's baby boy had made her yearn to start a family with Angel, though they had agreed to wait a year and just enjoy each other first.

"My cousin Bella is great. I am so glad I reached out to her. She promised to visit around New Year's."

"That's great," Marsha replied, picking at the salad she had brought to eat for lunch. It was a garden salad with no meat or cheese and low-fat dressing. She was ever battling the twenty pounds she had not been able to successfully drop since giving birth to her twin sons fourteen years earlier. It seemed a futile battle.

"So," Jemma broached the touchy subject of Marsha's soon-to-be ex-husband, Dr. Troy Fields. "How are things progressing with the divorce?"

"It's not. We've been at a standstill all summer. He won't budge on my
demands."

"That's ridiculous. You are only asking for what is fair and what you are rightfully entitled to."

That was true. Well, at least in her opinion. Her husband had walked out on her six months ago and moved in with his new girlfriend, Nancy. More like Barbie, Marsha thought. The blonde was at least ten years younger than her thirty-six, and incredibly fit. Blue eyes, perfect hair and skin. She actually looked like a Barbie doll. She didn't really know the woman, didn't want to, and who could blame her. The woman had been sleeping with a married man.

But Troy was no prize, Marsha thought. He was grouchy, tired all the time, well, now she knew why. He had an affair once before, and they had worked through it for the sake of their children, but apparently, he was a pattern cheater. Other women had come to her since she had announced the divorce and told her that they had seen him out with numerous women over the years. It had been humiliating, to say the least, and was doing a number on her self-esteem. She shook off those thoughts and focused her energy on her anger and her new living situation these past two weeks.

"Right. I want child support. Not much. No alimony even though I worked while he was in med school. I just want the fifty thousand he took out of our checking account to put the down payment on his condo in San Antonio for him and his girlfriend. And half the proceeds of the house in Medina we paid off last year." Marsha had moved into Angel's ranch house. Since he moved in with Jemma before the wedding this summer, he had offered to rent it to her and sell it to her if she wanted. And she did want the beautiful property. She liked the ranch life. She had grown up on a ranch not too far away and missed the simple life. She had always hated the suburbs. But Troy had wanted to live in town in a big, fancy old home that she had spent years fixing up.

"Why is he being so difficult about this?" Jemma took a bite of the apple she had brought to eat after she finished her yogurt.

"I don't know. He makes a great income, but I think it might be the girlfriend. She seems to have expensive taste. Plus, Troy says he paid for most of the repairs and the house payments over the years, but I was the one doing the fixing up and taking care of the children and working, while he was out carousing."

"I'm sure the judge will see it your way."

13

"We have to do mediation first. Court ordered before we can bring it to the judge."

Jemma nodded and took another bite before she broached her Labor Day party topic again. "So, will you come to the barbecue? I think it would be good for you to be around some new people. The boys are with Troy for the weekend, right?"

Yes, she thought, and with Barbie, er, Nancy, she internally self-corrected. It was not like her to be so petty. "I don't know," Marcy hedged. "I was going to go to my sister Lena's and spend a little time with my nieces before I have to pick up the boys from Troy's condo. Her husband, Jimmy, is out of town. She doesn't live very far from him."

"Oh, phooey. Come to my barbecue and make him drop off the boys. You need a little fun. Plus, there will be lots of new people from the TVFD. Pops said he had a bunch of new recruits."

"I'll think about it."

"Don't think. Just do."

"Great advice coming from a science teacher." Marcy laughed.

"You are not my student. You're my friend." Jemma reached across the table and gave Marcy's hand a squeeze.

"I promise to think about it, but I am too old to be set up with some hunky young volunteer firefighter."

"Marcy, thirty-six isn't old. You are still young and beautiful. You have gorgeous brown hair. Your eyes are like emeralds. You've got curves. Please, there will be guys lining up to get your attention."

"Jemma!" Marcy exclaimed, shocked. "I'm not looking for attention just yet."

Jemma shook her head. "No way, sister. You have to come. You don't have to act on anything, but it will do you good." Jemma knew Marcy needed to realize a lot of men would find her attractive. The separation and the cheating, over-critical husband, had done a number on Marcy. This was exactly what she needed.

"I don't know. I just," Marcy laughed nervously, "don't think I am ready to jump out of the frying pan straight into the fire yet."

"Well, I think you should." Jemma gave her a serious expression from across the breakroom table.

"I will think about it," Marcy reiterated, knowing it was a promise she would not be able to keep. Her job, her boys, were all she needed. She knew finding a man at her age and with her baggage, physical and other-wise, would be no easy task. So she lied to herself, telling herself she didn't really want it, anyway.

CHAPTER 4

Blake sat outside on his balcony and sipped a cold beer. He cracked open the cold case file he had decided to focus his attention on first. The victim was Cole Lansing, a San Antonio artist whose body was discovered in the desert beyond William's Creek. Hikers had discovered the body three years ago. Dental records had been used to identify the human remains, and they connected the case to a missing person's report from two years prior.

The victim, forty years old, had been reported missing by his young wife. They had no children. The man had one brother who resided in North Carolina. Their parents lived in Austin. Lansing had been a well-established painter and sculptor. He had gotten national attention for his work and was frequently commissioned by artsy types in California and the casinos in Vegas. He was well-off and left a grieving widow with financial stability.

The hikers had sat for lunch, and one of the duo

had kicked a rock to make a clearing for the picnic. Underneath lay the man's skull. The hiker reported, "I found this skull looking right at me." They made their way back to their campsite and called authorities once they had cell service.

Forensics had been led to the spot of the discovery and had painstakingly picked over the scene, collecting all of the fragments of bone and debris that could possibly be evidence in the crime. But other than bits of decayed cloth and bone, nothing of note had turned up. The medical examiner had been able to piece together the cause of death from what little remained. None of it had been good. The examiner concluded that there had been extensive trauma and the cause of death had been violent. Broken and fractured bones and sharp gouges on the bones of the chest and hands led the medical examiner to conclude the man had been stabbed to death several dozen times with a sharp hunting knife. He had also been cracked on the head with a large, heavy object.

The deputy investigator at the time concluded that someone had probably knocked him out somewhere, brought him out to the desert where he finished the job, and then buried him. There were no traces of evidence that linked to a killer.

The investigator found no viable suspects. Of course, the wife had been their prime suspect. By all accounts, however, the newly married couple were extremely happy, and the grieving woman had been part of the search for over a year before the body was discovered. The man did not owe money to anyone, nor did he have a single enemy. The trail had gone cold, if there had even been one.

Though it seemed unlikely he would find the culprit, it was Blake's job to try. Sometimes, even five years later, memories could be jogged or people wanted to talk about things they found too preposterous to mention in the moment. He would start by checking in with the wife and the neighbors, then widen the circle to the business contacts.

Blake flipped a page to the missing person's case. When the young wife reported her husband missing, police were dispatched to her home to take the report. She'd reported her husband had gone to Las Vegas where he had been commissioned to do a mural for one of the casinos, but he had never shown up. In fact, the plane ticket had never been used. His vehicle was found at the airport. Security camera footage of the entrance to the airport hadn't picked him up in the building or directly outside which proved Cole Lansing never made it inside. Blake decided to do a search of crimes committed around the airport during the months before and after the man's disappearance. Perhaps he had been grabbed in the parking lot. If it had been a robber out to steal the man's money, or even a serial killer, a pattern of those crimes may have emerged after the fact.

He did not want to leave any stone unturned.

CHAPTER 5

Marcy left the mediation office in disgust. How dare Troy! He had threatened to sue for custody of the boys. She knew he did not want that. Heck, he didn't even want partial custody. He was perfectly content with the current arrangement, alternating holidays and every other weekend, with promises of trips to be taken during the summer. She did not begrudge him that at all. He did love his kids, but he did not have the time daily to supervise their homework, their baseball practices, and other extracurricular events with his surgeon's schedule. This was his way of trying to make her concede on not asking for the money from their depleted checking account and fifty percent of the proceeds from the sale of the house.

"Marsha, wait!" Troy trotted across the street after her. She hated the way he said her name. She much preferred to be called Marcy, always had. He never cared.

"For what, Troy? Some other ridiculous demand?"

"Marsha, I want this done as much as you do, but I do not have that kind of money just lying around."

"Once the house sells, you can pay me from the proceeds. It's not my fault you spent everything we had saved on your new condo and that ridiculous car." Last weekend she had seen him leave the boys' baseball conditioning in a new BMW, a two-seater no less. She supposed his Land Rover was not good enough for Barbie!

As if on cue, Marcy saw Troy glance behind him. He saw Nancy pull up in his newest purchase and he smiled and waved at her affectionately. He gave her a sign to wait. She waved back and gave Marcy a huge grin. Her lips, painted cherry red, cracked, revealing bright super white teeth. Everything about her was perfect, Marcy groaned inwardly. "Nice car," Marcy said flippantly. She had gotten to keep the Chevy Malibu in the separation. It had been the older of their two vehicles.

"Nancy wanted a BMW for her birthday." He gave Marcy a sheepish smile. The one he used with her often when he bought something extravagant without telling her. "Sorry, I told Nancy to pick me up on Mercer Avenue. I didn't want to, um, you know, make things uncomfortable for you."

"Why would seeing Nancy make me uncomfortable?" Marcy lied. She yanked down her blouse self-consciously. Nancy had gotten out of the car and was leaning against it, reapplying her lipstick using a small compact mirror. Her short glittery tank top revealed a flat stomach.

"No reason, I guess." His eyes strayed to her blouse and what she had been trying to hide. The last five years or so he had harped on her enough about the twenty pounds she had never been able to shed after the boys had been born.

"Exactly. I have no reason to be jealous. And I'm not jealous. So, what do you want?" Marcy snapped. She had not been able to keep the irritation out of her voice, no matter how hard she tried.

Troy sighed and held out his hands as he spoke in supplication. "Listen, Marsha, you and I hadn't been getting along for years. Don't blame Nancy."

Flabbergasted, Marcy could not find the words to speak. "No, of course not. Why would I bring Nancy into this? Blame her? She's just the woman for whom you decided to abandon your family." She watched as Nancy put her lipstick into her handbag and took out her cell phone. One lean leg crossed over the other as she fiddled with her phone.

My goodness, she really does look like a Barbie doll, Marcy thought. The woman across the street in a short tight designer skirt was beautiful with tan, long legs. She was everything Marcy was not. From even this distance, she could see her manicured nails, her hair professionally cut and styled. The clothes expensive. The heels she wore with her outfit, Christian Louboutin, cost more than she made in a month.

"Jealousy doesn't look good on you, Marsha," Troy remarked sardonically. Marcy had the urge to wipe the smirk off his face with her hand.

"I told you. I'm not jealous. It just doesn't help when

she shows up in a fancy new car you paid for when I can't even pay my rent on time." And it was true. She had to ask Angel to wait a few days this past month until her paycheck cleared. She was angrier about her frozen accounts than she was about Troy's latest conquest. She hated asking her friends to wait even if it had been only a few days.

"Your friends will wait. They know you'll be good for it."

His remarks only served to increase her ire. She gripped her keys tighter in the palm of her hand. "Yes, true, but they shouldn't have to. You didn't need to leave me high and dry, living paycheck to paycheck."

He sighed. "Listen, I just did what my lawyer told me to do. He recommended I do it before I served you because you would do it."

"You know me better than that. Nice lawyer, by the way. Real prize winner there." She didn't even attempt to keep the sarcasm from her voice.

"I'll talk to Rudy," Troy stated in an indulgent tone of voice, as if he were doing her a favor. She had heard this before. "I won't fight for custody if you will let go of the idea of getting anything from selling the house in Banderas. I'll give you the fifty thousand from the checking account. That will be plenty for a down payment on the ranch, and you could get a mortgage. We, er, well, you, have stellar credit."

"That house was just as much mine as it was yours. You may have paid the bills, but the work I put into making it a home for the boys, for you, counts. I won't budge on that. God, Troy, I could easily ask for alimony and get it. Everyone says so, but I don't want that. I don't want anything from you but what is owed to me, and your promise to take equal responsibility in the boys' college expenses if they choose to go."

"You're being unreasonable."

She worked hard to keep from screaming. "Me? I'm being unreasonable! You make a great salary. Really, at forty, you have lots of years ahead of you. You have great investments. Why? Why are you being so difficult?"

"All my money is tied up, you know that. I need cash to start my new life with Nancy."

"Gold-digger," Marcy muttered.

He blew her off. "You can think that, but she's not a gold-digger. You don't know her. Yes, she likes nice things, and I like to give them to her, but she's got her own money, too. We're going in this as equals."

Marcy felt like she had been slapped. His look told her, in not so many words, that she wasn't his equal. He implied he married down.

"How dare you?" she murmured low in her voice when a wave of blonde hair caught her attention. She glanced at Nancy, who smirked at her from across the street, then had the audacity to wave. Her hand sparkled in the late Texas summer sun with the huge diamond ring she sported. They were engaged, and Nancy clearly wanted her to know it! Marcy removed Troy's hand from her car door and opened it. "Listen, we're done here. I have places to be," she lied.

"Fine, go. Don't be late picking up the boys Monday night," he threw her way before turning on his expensive Italian leather-shoed heel and crossing the busy street as if he owned it. She was never late picking up the boys. How dare he make it sound otherwise!

He's such an entitled ass, Marcy thought as she watched him wrap his arms around Nancy and kiss her. He'd always been a bit of a snob and more so as the years passed. Troy kissed Nancy with passion, and she knew he was putting on a show for her benefit, trying to hurt her. It did, but it didn't. She didn't love him and hadn't for a long time. Yes, she was angry. But that was because she had been dutiful, playing her part for the children. For them, she had stayed long after she probably should have. She shook her head and started the car. She made the U-turn into traffic when there was a break. Again, Nancy waved, and again, Marcy saw the ring sparkling and knew Troy had spent a mint on it for his new trophy girlfriend. Correction. Fiancée. He was all about show. He spent every dime he made and would have during their marriage had she not insisted he invest some. He was well off, but cash poor.

Grr! She hit the gas as she turned out of town onto the highway. She wanted nothing more than to curl up on her outdoor swing with a glass of wine, a good book, and listen to the night sounds of Texas. Yes, she had things to do, and none of them concerned spending another pointless moment arguing with her soon-to-be ex.

Marcy made the hour and a half drive from San Antonio to the ranch. Though it was a bit further out than her house in Medina to her job at the high school, it would be a nice thirty-minute drive spent bonding with her kids. Austin and Adam would be a captive audience, and she wouldn't have to corner them to find out about their lives at school. Like most teenagers, her two sons were growing up and did not enjoy talking with their parents about things like school and their friends.

Because they were spending this last week before school started with their father, she got to enjoy the drive alone that evening. After leaving the mediation, she had gone to the school to finish setting up her classroom and then had a quick bite with Calliope, one of Jemma's closest friends, and another science teacher at the school. Marcy had spotted her leaving the building and invited her out. It seemed a better idea than cooking for herself that evening. Catching up with Calliope since the last time they saw each other at Jemma's wedding provided a much-needed distraction.

As she turned onto the dirt road leading to the ranch she now called home, the sun sank low in the western skies. She loved it here. The solitude. The quiet. Much better than the big house her husband insisted they buy in town. She thought about the days ahead. The days without her boys when they went to be with their dad and how she would fill her time. Maybe she'd write that book she had always been hankering to write. Her love of books went beyond teaching them to her high school English and creative writing students.

Nope. She did not miss her old house. The huge home was too much for her and the kids. They were growing up and loved the outdoors. They needed the wide-open spaces to explore that piqued their curiosity and got them away from the electronics. She had plans to get some animals, maybe even a dog for the boys. Some chickens, a goat. That would be nice. She would have the animals to keep her company, and she would fill beautiful days writing outside on the wide porch. Her future still looked bright. She didn't need a man in her life. She pulled up close to the house and got out of her car, feeling much better than she had that afternoon.

She fiddled with one hand inside her purse for the key to open the door, while simultaneously swinging open the outer door, when the resounding sound of glass shattering filled her ears. In almost the same moment, the hairs on the back of her neck rose, then something hard hit her from behind on the back of the head. The excruciating pain made her world turn black. She did not even feel the ground when it rose up to hit her in the face as she crumpled to the porch.

CHAPTER 6

Blake knocked on numerous doors in the San Antonio neighborhood where the once renowned artist, Cole Lansing, had lived with his widow. The woman across the street provided what little information he knew so far.

"No, sir. She does not live there anymore. Moved out about four years ago. Not too long after that poor man's body was found."

"How long after?" Blake asked the woman who had come outside to speak with him.

"About six months or so, I guess, give or take."

"Hmm, okay. Did you know Cole or his wife, Noreen?"

"No, not really. Only in passing. She was awfully young for him, though. But she was pretty enough. Friendly. She waved when she went to get the mail, but never stayed long enough to have a conversation."

Blake checked his notes. Noreen had been twenty-two at the time, according to his records.

"Did it seem strange to you that she left so soon after her husband's body was recovered?" he asked, hoping the neighbors had gossiped and she had heard some of it.

"Well, some of the neighbors thought not too highly of her after that. You know how rumors go. But her brother had come to live with her for a while. I talked to him a time or two. He wasn't so nice. They fought a lot. I guess siblings do that. I could never make out what it was about. He told me her folks wanted her to come back home. I assume that's why she ended up moving."

"Do you know where home was for her and her brother?" Blake asked.

"He said they were from California once," the older woman said, and he could tell she was thinking back. Her eyes came back into focus with a retrieved memory. "There was this one time the brother said they were from Oregon. But she had said something about living in California. When I questioned him, he said they lived most of their lives in California but then had moved to Oregon, so I suspect that is where they went."

"Thank you, Mrs. Meade. I appreciate the information. One more question. What was the brother's name? I don't have it in my records."

"His name was Charles, or Carl. I heard her call out to him by both of those names."

Carl, a shortened version of Charles. He jotted it down and would put it in the notes on his phone.

"Thank you again." He was about to leave the porch when Mrs. Meade stopped him.

"I'm sorry I could not be of more help. If you want more information, she did have one girlfriend. Her name was Lisa. She works down at the Anytime Fitness Center on York Avenue, I believe. My son uses that gym and he kind of had a crush on her, but don't tell her I told you that."

Blake smiled at the older woman. "I promise not to say a word."

None of the other neighbors recalled anything useful. Many of the neighbors had only recently moved into the area.

Blake sat in his car to contemplate his next move and made a note to check the whereabouts of Noreen Lansing and her brother Charles in California and Oregon. He would like to have a conversation with the widow to see if she recalled anything about her husband's disappearance after so much time had passed.

It was still early in the day. He could head over to some of the local artists' hangouts, but decided he might be better off trying the gym and looking for Lisa. He would save the hangouts until later that evening when more artists might be in attendance.

Blake did a quick search of the local fitness centers, and the location where Lisa worked was the first to appear on his GPS. It was five minutes away. He tapped the navigation button and the route appeared on his screen. He followed it.

* * *

"Hi. Yes, I am that Lisa," the petite brunette gushed. She was pretty, short, around twenty-seven years of age, Blake estimated. "Are you looking for a personal trainer?"

Blake smiled. "No, I'm not. I'm here on official police business." He flashed his badge. Her bottom lip dropped in a cute pout.

"Oh, that's too bad. I could have really given you a good workout."

Blake snickered, catching the woman's double entendre. "Sorry, sweetie. I'm working a cold case. The Cole Lansing case. I was actually looking for Noreen. Her neighbors said she moved. Sold everything and then left about six months after his remains were discovered."

Lisa's face changed then. Sadness filled her eyes. "Cole was so nice. Noreen was sad for a really long time."

"Yes, it was quite the tragedy. We haven't given up finding who murdered him. That's why I wanted to talk to Noreen. See if maybe she remembered something from that time."

Lisa sighed. "We were so close. We were friends before she met Cole. I was a bridesmaid in her wedding ceremony at City Hall. I met her at the YMCA a few months after she moved to town."

"Have you remained in touch? Do you have an address? Phone number?"

"No. She must have changed her number when she

moved. I tried calling her a few times, but the number I had for her was assigned to a different person."

"That's kind of odd," Blake remarked to see if it would bring forth any gossip from the trainer.

"I thought so, too. But it happens. She probably wanted to forget all about her time here. Reporters were hounding her. I thought she would at least keep in touch with me, yet I have not heard from her at all. We did everything together. We ran together every day. Pilates three times a week. Went shopping. But nope. Not a single phone call or text."

Another dead end, Blake thought. However, he did find it odd she didn't stay in touch with her closest friend. It could be as Lisa suggested and she did not want to remember this painful chapter of her life.

"It could be what you are saying. But what about her brother? Do you have his contact information, perchance? Maybe he didn't change his number."

"He was a jerk. So bossy. No, I never had Corey's number. I didn't like him one bit. He was always telling his sister what to do."

"Did you say his name was Corey?"

"I guess it was Charles, but she called him Corey, sometimes Carl."

The guy had an awful lot of nicknames, Blake thought. He didn't know if he was chasing his own tail or making something out of nothing.

"Well, thank you, Lisa." Blake handed her his card. "Please call me if you think of anything or if she reaches out to you."

"You are very welcome."

Lisa slipped the card into her cell phone case as he left. Maybe he'd get lucky at the different artists' hang-outs. It was time to find a new angle.

CHAPTER 7

Marcy called Jemma the moment she regained consciousness on the porch. Darkness had descended. Her head hurt like a son-of-a-bitch, and from the amount of blood on the porch and the stickiness on the back of her head, she must have a serious gash. Her head spun, but she managed to find her purse lying at her feet. Her wallet was missing, but thankfully her cell phone was still inside.

Shocked, Jemma declared, "I'm calling you an ambulance. Don't drive anywhere. Angel and I will meet you at the hospital."

"Okay. Okay," Marcy murmured in the darkness. The typical night sounds edged into her awareness. She realized now they hadn't been there when she had arrived. So foolish. She should have been more alert as she approached the door. She needed to install a flood-light and motion detector.

"Stay on the phone with her, Jemma," she heard Angel say in the background. "I'll make the call and send someone from the TVFD to do transport. I'll call the police, too."

Marcy wasn't thinking straight. She should have called 911 herself. Feeling woozy, she found enough energy to lock herself in her car as Jemma talked to her the whole time. Eventually, she heard sirens in the distance.

Once in the ambulance, only then did Jemma end the call. She and Angel were already en-route to the hospital Jemma told her. "We will be there soon. Do you want me to call your sister? Troy?" Jemma asked.

"No. I don't want to worry anyone," Marcy replied.

"Okay," Jemma promised before she hung up.

Once at the hospital everything happened like a blur around her. A doctor on call told her she needed stitches, then a nurse came in to wash out her wounds after pictures were taken for the police to see when they arrived moments later.

"Please let me stitch her up before you start with the questions, Deputy," the doctor warned the young man who held a notepad and pen. "Here and here." The doctor ordered the nurse to apply numbing medication so she didn't feel the thread and needle. Marcy already had an IV in and pain medication given to her, but she did not recall seeing someone do it.

"Can I come in, Doctor?" Jemma peered into the room from the open doorway. "She called us." Jemma indicated Angel behind her. "We are her closest friends in the area. Her family is in San Antonio."

"If it's okay with the patient, it's okay with me," the

doctor answered. "Just keep to that side of the room until the nurse and I finish stitching her up."

Marcy nodded, and winced when she felt something tug on her head. The doctor chuckled. "Don't move, sweetheart. Use your words," he spoke to her like a child.

She felt Jemma gently clasp her hand, and she gave it a squeeze. "Thanks for coming. I appreciate it."

"Of course. Of course."

"Almost done," the doctor announced. "Just a few more. I do want some X-rays done of your skull to make sure nothing is wrong, Mrs. Fields, but if you feel up to it, the deputy is chomping at the bit to get his questions answered."

"Yes, of course, Doctor," Marcy responded. She felt more clearheaded as the IV did its magic.

To the deputy the doctor directed his next words. "Ten minutes, they will be here to bring her down for X-rays. She's got some pain medicine in her, though, and more coming in, so she may not be awake for too much longer."

"Gotcha, Doc."

Jemma and Angel listened to Marcy describe what happened to her to the deputy. Angel, beside her, fumed. "I'll put in some floodlights and motion detectors. A whole security system. This won't happen again. Not on my watch."

"We have guys at the scene," Deputy Rodriguez assured them. "My partner is there. Whoever did this didn't even get into the house. Maybe a drug addict. Looks like your wallet was the only thing taken. The fact that he did not go into the house sounds like a snatch and grab, though it seems weird all the way out on your ranch, but maybe that was what he was counting on. We are scouting the property looking for tire tracks now."

"I'm glad they, or whoever it was, that did this did not get into the house. I just finished settling all our stuff inside."

"Just the door broken, and well, your head, ma'am."

"I'm going to be tightening up security for you there," Angel declared.

"This isn't your fault, Angel." Marcy looked at her friend's husband and saw guilt in his expression.

"Thanks, but you are a woman alone out there. I should have thought of that. When I lived there, my dog always let me know when someone was coming up the road. Maybe you should get a dog. I know a guy who has two chocolate lab pups that need a home. Labradors are a good breed around kids."

"Yes, actually I did want to get a dog. Do you think I can take them both? One for each of the boys."

"Absolutely. They should be ready to leave their mom in a week or two. I'll bring them out myself. Make sure they have all their shots and a clean bill of health."

"Thank you, Angel. The boys will be thrilled."

"You don't have to thank me."

Jemma glanced at her husband. She knew he felt responsible for what happened to Marcy. He had berated himself in the car the whole ride to the hospital after she had hung up with Marcy.

Before Marcy knew it, a technician came and escorted her to get the X-rays the doctor had ordered. By the time she returned she felt much improved.

Jemma had news. "The doctor said we can take you home tonight if you like, but you should probably not be alone. Unless you want to stay in the hospital. Angel and I wouldn't feel right if you went back to the ranch tonight. How about sleeping at our place tonight?"

"I don't have any clothes to wear."

"You can wear some of my sweats and sleep t-shirts tonight. Then tomorrow, Angel will swing by your place first thing in the morning and get enough stuff for you for the entire weekend. He really doesn't want you going back until after he installs the security system, floodlights, and motion detectors."

"I could stay with my sister."

"If you would prefer that, we could drive you to San Antonio." Jemma looked upset. Though Marcy did not want to impose, she reluctantly agreed. She didn't want to worry her sister either.

"Wonderful." Jemma clapped her hands. "This way you have to come to the Labor Day barbecue."

Marcy groaned but laughed at the same time. "This was your plan all along wasn't it?"

"Not the crack on the head part, but yes. Yes, it was," Jemma teased in return.

CHAPTER 8

On his day off, Blake headed into the office to do more digging on the hot yoga establishment for his current case. He was planning on working the Lansing case during the week. A few other deputies were in the office, and they were working on a new case that had come in last night.

"Hey, New York! Got a minute?" Rodriguez asked. "I want to get your input on this case."

"Sure. What's up?"

Rodriguez told him about a home invasion in Banderas the previous evening. "The woman of the house was coming home from work pretty late. Just starting to get dark. She gets hit from behind just as she unlocks the front door. They grabbed her wallet and then took off."

"Smash and grab sounds like a drug addict to me," Blake gave his opinion. "They didn't go into the house?"

"Nope. It was locked up pretty tight. No evidence the perp or perps made it into the house."

"If they knocked her out and didn't try to get her keys or car, then I say drug addict looking for a few quick bucks for a fix. But this ain't New York, so you tell me, what are you thinking?"

"It sounds like a drug addict is the best-case scenario, but all the way out on one of the ranches? That is a long way to roam to look for a fix. In town, maybe, but I don't know. They didn't try to get into the house, and we are looking for tire tracks, but so far haven't seen any but hers and what looks like the property owner's."

"I'm sure you will figure it out," Blake said. "How much cash did the lady have on her?"

"About a hundred and fifty," Rodriguez said. "Some credit cards."

"Put a trace on them, yet?"

"Already done. It sure does seem like a drug addict."

"Sounds about right," Blake agreed. "No prints?"

"We took prints off the door and porch. Hopefully, we get a hit on the them."

"No cameras?"

"Nope. 'Fraid not. A lot of the bigger operations have them, but not the smaller places. The property owner is planning on installing some cameras, though. He is renting the place to the victim and her two kids."

"Good idea." A woman alone should have some sort of security, Blake had always felt. "Well, sounds like you are doing what you can. Victim gonna be okay?"

"Yes, she was released from the hospital last night.

She was fortunate not to have her kids for the evening. They were at the ex's."

"Yes, that was a good thing. No telling what he would have done to the kids or the trauma they would have suffered seeing their mom accosted."

"Definitely. We hope to catch the bastard. No hits on her cards, though. She has cancelled them and ordered new ones by now. But the guy might still try to use them after he blows through his high on the cash."

"True. I gotta talk to Riggs. Good luck finding the bastard," Blake offered in parting.

Blake found Jack on the phone. He was scowling but held up a hand for Blake to wait. "Sorry to hear that, Pops. Go do your thing."

"Everything all right?" Blake asked.

"Yeah, no. Pops has a fire to put out. The TVFD is going to be busy today."

"Sorry to hear it."

"His guys and gals will handle it. It's what they trained for. What you will be training for," Jack reminded him.

"Yes, already got my paperwork in, and I'll begin training soon."

"Good, now what ya got for me?" Blake filled him in. "Sounds like you're making the right calls. Talk to Penelope about that new hot yoga place. I heard she goes there."

"Penelope?"

"Yeah, TVFD, you met her when you dropped off your paperwork last night."

"So, you already knew I dropped off the papers."

"I got my ear to the ground. Small towns in Texas have their advantages, New York."

"That they do," Blake replied, then headed back to his desk to make some calls.

He took up the packet of papers Pops had given him and rifled through the ones he hadn't had time to read yet. He did recall Pops saying it had a phone tree of all the volunteers. He found Penelope's number and called it. She picked up after the first ring.

"Hello."

"Hey, Penelope. It's Blake Levine. We met the other night when I came to drop off some paperwork at the fire department in Tarpley."

"Sorry, New York. I'm taken."

Go figure his new nickname was already making the rounds, but he also had to laugh at her quick reply that she was taken. She was a good-looking woman, and he supposed a lot of the new volunteers might take a crack at her. He liked her straightforwardness.

Blake laughed. "Sorry, Penelope. It's not that you aren't cute as a button. It's business. Jack told me to call you about a case I'm working on. I need some information about the hot yoga place in Banderas. I'm looking for a person who was wearing one of their t-shirts."

"Okay, sure."

"Just wondering if you heard any rumors about a patron there who might be having some serious troubles with someone. A woman wearing one of their neon green t-shirts was looking to hire a killer to take someone out."

"Shit!"

"Yeah, I know."

"Hope you catch her. I've seen lots of the green tank tops around. I don't really stay and talk with the other members much, but I can keep my ear to the ground for you. If I hear anything, I'll let you know."

"Thanks. I don't have anyone on the inside, so that'd be great. I'm going to talk to the owner but don't want to give too much away. Keep my case on the down-low as much as you can."

"No problem. Good luck."

"Thanks. I'll let you get back to work."

"Okay. See you tomorrow and Thursday next week."

"Wait. What? Tomorrow? And next week?"

"The barbecue tomorrow at Angel and Jemma's and Thursday night is a class for the new trainees. I am doing the show and tell on equipment. It was in the packet that Pops gave you."

Oh, shit. The packet he hadn't read yet. He flipped a few more pages until he saw important dates. Darn, if he did not have a ton of shit to add to the calendar on his phone. His down time had just significantly decreased. It looked like he would pretty busy over the next few months. The list of events and classes for the fall was two pages long. Well, he wanted to get to know the people in the community. And from the looks of it, he would start getting to know them tomorrow. There was a barbecue at one of the other volunteers' homes for Labor Day. An Angel Murphy with a Tarpley address.

"Thanks for the heads up."

"Sure thing, New York."

Blake needed to grab some stuff to make his killer potato salad for the barbecue tomorrow, but he wanted to run by the hot yoga establishment and talk to the manager if he could. He knew they were open by doing a Google search. As he was getting ready to leave, one of the guys passed by his desk and asked him if he wanted to have lunch with him and some of the guys in town. It was early. He glanced at his watch and told them to give him an hour and he'd meet them there.

Rodriguez gave him the particulars of a barbecue place in town they liked to frequent. It was near the hot yoga place, just two blocks down which made it convenient for him.

"See you in an hour, Rodriguez."

He locked his files in a cabinet and grabbed his keys off his desk.

* * *

A bell tinkled when Blake walked into the hot yoga establishment. A bubbly brunette greeted him to the right while several people shopped in the small store behind her for merchandise.

"Looking to sign up?" the girl asked without looking up from her phone. She looked to be about seventeen.

"No, thanks. I just wanted to talk to the owner or a manager." He flashed his badge when the girl looked up.

The girl put her phone down. "Sure. She's here

today. I'll go get her. And she's both. The owner and the manager," the girl said over her shoulder as she passed him and went to a set of double glass doors that led to the classrooms. "I'll be right back."

It wasn't even a minute later when a taller woman with fiery red hair entered the lobby with the little brunette in tow. "He's right there, Mom."

The mother rolled her eyes at her teenaged daughter. She could clearly see he was right there. Blake laughed. Other than two shoppers, both women, and two other women sitting at the juicing station, he was the only other person and male present in the room. The women eyeballed him while pretending to shop or sip on their juices since he announced his identity. He saw their interest piqued, whether by him or the fact he was investigating something, he didn't know.

Gotta love small towns, he mused.

One woman gave him a complete head to toe once over. He smiled. The woman sipping the green juice was pretty, but blondes were not really his thing. Not anymore.

"Hi. I'm Mika," the redhead introduced herself. "Amani, looks like those women are ready with their purchases. Be sure and get those two boxes out of the storage area for me when you are finished."

"Sure, Mom."

"Come," the woman beckoned. "Let's go to my office away from prying eyes."

"Absolutely." He didn't want to advertise his reason for being there anymore than did the owner. He followed Mika to her office, passing four full classes in session.

"You're doing well," he remarked. Several women and a few men were wearing some neon tank tops.

"Yes, thankfully. I knew this business would do well. People have been wanting something different for a while. You know, different from what a typical gym offers, and I've always felt yoga was great for fitness. Hot yoga is even better. It's strenuous enough to burn some major calories, yet relaxing as well as healthy. It's amazing really. Have you tried it?" Mika asked as she opened the door to her office and ushered him in.

"No." Blake laughed as he watched her sit behind her desk. She indicated the chair facing it. He took a seat. "I don't think so."

Her eyebrow arched. "It's great for men, too, even men as large as you. You'll be more balanced and your already great physique will stay toned while your flexibility will increase."

Beneath a great sales pitch, he heard the undercurrent and insinuation and smiled at Mika. She must be a single mom. At least, with the insinuation there, he hoped so. He didn't begrudge the new, aggressive woman who went after what she wanted. But damn, these Texas women were just as aggressive as any woman from New York. He, though, preferred a bit of a chase. "I'm actually here on a case I am working on." He flipped open a notebook he slipped from his pocket.

"Okay," Mika pronounced, looking confused.

"It's an active case so I can't go into too much detail. I just wanted to ask about your merchandise. I am looking for a woman who was seen wearing one of your tops."

"A criminal?" she asked.

Again, he didn't want to give too much away. "I'm not sure, but someone with information I need for my case. I am also asking you not to discuss the case with anyone as it is ongoing."

"So, a witness then?" When he didn't comment, Mika continued. "Of course. I won't say a word." Intrigued, she waited for him to tell her more.

Blake continued, "She was seen in Tarpley wearing one of your t-shirts, actually a tank top to be exact."

"Oh, dear!"

"What?" Her reaction to his comment was startled.

"I'm afraid I had over one thousand tank tops made. I gave over five hundred away as a marketing strategy before we even opened at various events throughout the area. The rest I gave to some of the employees and trainers, and to every client who signed up for a monthly contract. I ordered orange, green, pink and yellow. Two hundred and fifty of each. We give them to anyone who signs up."

"How many did you give away to clients?" Blake asked, though he knew any one of 250 people, whether they worked, attended or not, could be the woman he was looking for. And even then, someone who had one of the tank tops may have given it away. But he always followed all leads. Even the tough ones.

"Three hundred and ninety to be exact. So about 110 were left from the marketing. The rest I gave to some of the employees and sold off months ago."

"Do you have any records of who got what color? Sizes?"

"Probably only the ones we sold, I'm afraid."

"Can I get those records sent to me?" He handed her his card.

"Sure. Can I email them to you, Deputy?"

"Yes, that would be great. And if you could send me your client list that would be helpful, too." Five hundred names were a place to start. He had a fifty-fifty shot of the blonde being a woman on those lists. He needed to call Susie at The Depot and get the woman's approximate size. That could narrow down the list.

"First thing Monday, I'll have Janet get you the information. I'm sorry I couldn't be more help. Is this woman okay?" She was digging and Blake was glad he hadn't told her much, not even the color of the t-shirt he was looking for in particular.

"I'm really not at liberty to say. But you have been a great help, Mika. Thank you."

"Not at all, Deputy. We Texans like to help our men in uniform."

Blake left the yoga studio feeling as if he had made a little headway on his current case. It was all about digging and doing the legwork. It was true, he would have five hundred or so names to look into. Only half of what was out there. But it was something. Though, it also meant five hundred nameless, faceless people were wearing the tank top, and he hoped it wasn't one of them who wanted someone dead. But a lot of crimes were solved by following the paper trail, and that was what he would do in this case until the mystery woman tried again to hire someone. Come Monday he would have a ton of cross referencing to do. Detective work in New York was, if not nothing, tedious and grueling paperwork. Even in Texas, that didn't change.

CHAPTER 9

Over lunch with the two other deputies Blake discussed some of the cold cases he was working on while they chatted about the violent burglary that had gone awry the previous evening. Rodriguez and Logan had been on the scene.

Rodriguez had also questioned the victim in the hospital. "Mrs. Fields, such a sweet lady. We gotta catch this guy and put her worry and fears to rest."

"Yes," Logan agreed. "I don't blame her for moving after that prick of a husband left her. But I'm glad Angel's putting in that security system for her."

"Angel Murphy?" Blake asked.

"Yes, you know him?" Logan asked.

"Nope. But I'm headed to a barbecue at his place tomorrow. I joined the TVFD."

"Oh, good for you, man." Rodriguez pushed his plate away. They were almost done eating.

"Yeah, well, this one may get away from us," Logan stated none too happily. "Prints came back and we got nothing there. Mrs. Field's is gonna be my daughter's creative writing teacher this year, so I really would like to nail the SOB."

"Yeah, me, too," chimed in Rodriguez who left a tip on the table for the waitress. Blake and Logan added a few extra dollars. "Nothing I hate worse than a coward who would attack a woman."

"Same," Blake agreed. They got up from their seats on the outdoor patio where they had been served their lunch. "You guys going to this barbecue at Murphy's tomorrow?"

"Nope. We're both working," said Logan, "but you'll have fun and meet a lot of the other guys and the volunteers from Tarpley."

"Check on Marsha Fields for us, will you? She'll be there. Angel and Jemma, Angel's wife, insisted she stay with them over the weekend until the security system's in place," Rodriguez said.

"Will do," Blake promised.

After he left the guys, Blake headed to his apartment. It was a few blocks north. He had found it on the internet and wasn't disappointed when he arrived in Texas. It was small, but larger than his place in the city. The three-story structure had four apartments per floor. It was a convenient location for work and shopping. He didn't need to take his vehicle, but always did just in case he needed to do some legwork.

Overall, he had been satisfied with his move. He liked Banderas and its people. He hadn't been much for Broadway or bars in the city or museums. He liked sports and fishing and there was plenty of that here in

Texas. His folks were a quick plane ride away in Arizona.

Inside, he took off his jacket and tie and loosened his collar and grabbed a bottle of beer from the refrigerator. He knew he needed to head back out and do some serious shopping as he liked to cook and prepare his own meals. He hadn't bought much yet, other than some microwavable dinners and cold cuts and bread for sandwiches. But he wanted to shower and relax before he went back out to do his shopping and to get the ingredients for his famous potato salad to bring to the barbecue tomorrow. His mother taught him you never went to someone's house without contributing.

In the meantime, he plopped down on the sofa and reached for the file on the hot yoga murder-for-hire case. He looked over his written notes. The manager had given him all the information he had asked for and was sending him more on Monday. He would talk to the waitress and the biker again next week to see if they recalled anything else. He might even head over to The Depot a night or two to see if the blonde showed up again. It was a longshot, but you never knew. Criminals were often creatures of habit.

CHAPTER 10

Marcy felt much better by Sunday morning. Her headache had all but disappeared, though her scalp was still tender from the stitches. She had stopped taking the painkillers because on Saturday she had been wiped out, and Jemma and Angel had spent the day doting on her. Being waited on by her friends made her uncomfortable.

When Angel was given the green light to go oversee the installation of the new security system, she was relieved to have that put into place. She would be able to return to her home soon. The police had taken what evidence they could find and had cleared the scene. It would ease her mind a great deal having a security system of some kind. As of now the police were thinking it had been an addict looking for some quick cash. But it bothered her that whoever had hit her had wandered out to her ranch.

But, since she felt better, she offered to pitch in for

the preparations for the barbecue her friends were hosting on Labor Day. She was glad Jemma accepted her assistance while Angel was out.

Marcy sat at Jemma's big country table and chopped vegetables for the salads that would be tossed tomorrow. She also helped Jemma bake three apple, two cherry, and two blueberry pies. They were expecting a big turnout. Many members of the TVFD were coming with their significant others, and plenty single ones, too, Jemma teased.

"It'll be nice catching up with everyone," Angel declared. They had only recently returned from their honeymoon the week before.

"Yes, it will be," Jemma added, taking the last pie out of the oven and setting it on the table to cool before it was wrapped up for tomorrow's celebration.

"I'm going to go check on the smoker and set it up in the clearing by the creek. The pork and ribs will smoke overnight."

"Okay," Jemma said. "Be careful."

Marcy saw Jemma shudder. She must be recalling the time when she slipped into the creek during the tornado when a flash flood had caused the bank to collapse. Thankfully, Angel had come to her rescue in time.

"No worries, sweetie. You know the guys helped me to stabilize the land with the sea-wall we put in. Plus, the water is way down now that summer is almost over."

"What's next?" Marcy asked.

"Well, lots of folks will be bringing stuff, so I am not worried about making too many more sides. But how about helping me with the fruit salad?"

"Sure thing."

"Stay right there," Jemma warned when Marcy was about to get up to get the fruit from the refrigerator. "I'll bring everything to you."

Marcy shook her head, feeling like a burden. Jemma pulled out bags of grapes, strawberries, fresh blueberries, and containers of already cut up pineapple. She set them on the table and handed Marcy a knife.

"I'll wash the fruit, and you cut. Just slice the grapes in half, and quarter the strawberries and toss them in the big green bowl. I'll chill it overnight and then we can add the whipped cream tomorrow."

"I do love that fruit salad."

"Oh, shoot! I forgot to buy the whipped cream. I'll have to add that to the list. Angel will run out later to the store to get the things I forgot."

"I can do that," Marcy offered. "Give you two a few hours alone." Her eyes twinkled mischievously. Jemma and Angel were still newlyweds, and she had been there all weekend.

"If you sure you feel up to it."

"Absolutely. You guys haven't let me do much, and frankly, I need to stretch my legs a bit."

"Okay."

She'd already told Jemma she was feeling better and had stopped taking the painkillers. "I will need to use your car, though. Mine is still in Banderas."

"No problem. The keys are hanging right there." Jemma pointed to the rack by the door.

Marcy finished helping Jemma with the fruit salad just as Angel arrived. "Ready with that list?" he asked, washing his hands in the sink.

"Actually, Marcy offered to go."

He was about to protest when he saw a familiar look in his wife's eyes.

"Um, okay." He mumbled the words quickly, and they laughed.

"Okay, I am outta here," Marcy teased, standing.

"Let me change that bandage before you go," Jemma offered, cleaning her hands in the sink.

Marcy sat back down and waited while Jemma parted her hair gently in the back where she got hit and the doctor had applied the stiches. "It looks like it's starting to heal," Jemma announced. "I don't think you really need the bandage. You can wash your hair tomorrow, too."

"I know. And I can't wait," Marcy said, standing again. "I've got to make an appointment to go to my doctor and get the stitches removed for the following Monday."

"I bet." Jemma walked her to the door.

The stitches were not water soluble so she was allowed to wash her hair. The doctor told her to wait a few days before doing so to allow enough of a scab to form. But he'd given her strict orders not to use shampoo for at least a week. A little conditioner was okay, but to be gentle around the gash. Jemma handed

Marcy a one-hundred-dollar bill and the list of items she needed. Marcy hated to take it, but money was tight right now because all of her accounts and assets were frozen. She only had access to one credit card. Other than it and the paycheck she received every two weeks, everything else was locked up tight until the divorce was settled.

* * *

Marcy walked up and down the aisles of the grocery store looking for all of the items on Jemma's list. She had gotten the marinade Jemma wanted for the ribs they were going to start smoking that evening, got the cans of beans and bacon, and hot dog and hamburger buns. She just needed some tomatoes and onions before heading over to get the whipped cream and ice cream.

Just as she grabbed a bag of onions, a hand clamped over hers and she jumped back in fright.

"Oh, excuse me," a deep voice rumbled from beside her. "I didn't mean to scare you."

Marcy stood back in shock. She hadn't even seen the man approach her, and he would be hard to miss. He was drop-dead gorgeous. Tall, dark, and handsome. His t-shirt clung to his toned body.

She was five feet eight and had to look up at the devastatingly handsome man standing beside her. His dark hair was damp from a recent shower and curled around his head. She licked her suddenly dry lips and quickly regained her composure. "No, I'm sorry I wasn't paying attention."

"No. It's my fault," the handsome stranger said. "I should have excused myself, but I didn't think you were gonna grab the same bag of onions as me. I really didn't mean to startle you like that."

Blake saw how startled the woman was by their hands touching while grabbing the same bag of onions. Her reaction was extreme, and she actually looked afraid. His police instinct kicked in and made him want to figure out why. And not just because she was stunning either. She was a classic beauty. She had pale skin and dark brown hair with glimmers of chestnut and gold in it. Her green eyes sparkled like sea glass twinkling on a sunlit beach. She was in her early to mid-thirties if he had to guess. He glanced at her hands. He didn't see a ring. Now, she was a possibility. He smiled.

"No apologies necessary," Marcy replied, though she found it hard to concentrate when he smiled. It had been a long time since a man had looked at her like that. She was shocked when she discerned desire in his brown eyes. A curl of heat warmed her lower belly, and to distract herself she handed the man the bag of onions. When his fingers touched hers and lingered momentarily, Marcy thought she would combust. Her head injury must be worse than she thought. She was having dirty fantasies about a man she just met in a grocery store in the produce aisle.

"Thank you," he said and placed the bag she had given him into his cart. When she blushed, Blake pulled his fingers away reluctantly. He looked over the brunette one more time. She had curves. More than a handful, and they were real. She had generous hips and a nice waistline. She wasn't a bony, slim exercise junky, but perfect. She was beautiful and carried herself like a woman who didn't try to be. She did appear sad, however. She had been the first woman to pique his interest since coming to Texas.

He observed her from lowered lashes as she reached for another bag of onions. Blake busied himself with selecting the potatoes he would need for his salad. He noticed her cart was full. She must be getting ready for some sort of Labor Day party or had a huge family. And he didn't know why the thought of her having a family, or rather being married, bothered him, but it did. He wanted to learn more about her. "You must be having a big party for Labor Day or you're shopping for a huge family," he remarked, using his detective skills to pry more information out of her. His cart was woefully empty. It was obvious he was single with his few selections. "You've got enough to feed an army here."

Marcy laughed as her nerves skittered. No one had flirted with her in a long time, or perhaps she had never noticed other men doing it at the time because she was married. But he was making her notice. She had never seen him before in this grocery store. His accent gave him away as a New Yorker. "My friend, Jemma, is having a barbecue tomorrow. I volunteered to pick up some things for her. My two sons are with their father. He has them every other weekend." Marcy intentionally filled in the blanks.

Again, with that smile. It curled her toes. "Oh, Jemma Murphy. I'll be at their barbecue tomorrow. In fact, that's why I'm here. Picking up the ingredients for potato salad. Never go emptyhanded, my mother taught me."

"She taught you right," Marcy agreed. She couldn't believe how easy it was to talk with a total stranger. A handsome one at that. She felt like she should end the conversation but didn't want to for some reason. Perhaps he was one of the new volunteers Jemma had mentioned to her only half a dozen times. He must have been reading her mind.

"I'm one of the new recruits. But, I'm also a deputy. Just hired. I moved here from New York."

She smiled in response. "Your accent gives you away."

"Guess I'm stuck with it."

"It's okay. I like it." She blushed at her unintentional confession.

"Well, I'm glad you like it. I'm also glad I met you because now I will know someone at the barbecue. It's hard for a single guy at these things, not knowing anyone. I'm Blake Levine, by the way." He offered his hand and let her know he was unattached at the same time.

"Marcy. Marcy Fields."

Blake recognized the name right away but didn't let on that he knew about her situation. Marcy Fields was the victim in Logan and Rodriguez's case. She had been hit on the head by a robber or drug dealer. He controlled his anger and worry for the woman who had been attacked coming home to her ranch. Fortunately, her two sons weren't with her. Every instinct to protect her rose within him. "It's nice to meet you. I'll see you at the barbecue, Marcy." He winked in parting.

Marcy's knees felt wobbly, and she knew it wasn't from the head injury.

CHAPTER 11

When Marcy returned from the grocery store, she noticed Angel's truck was gone and Jemma was alone in the kitchen.

Jemma went back outside with Marcy to help her finish unloading the groceries. Jemma grabbed as many bags as she could from the trunk. "Oh, the security company called from the ranch, and they were nearly finished. Angel had to run over there to sign the papers and learn how to operate the system. He'll explain it all to you when he gets back later."

"Good. It gives us a chance to talk. You'll never believe what happened to me at the grocery store."

"What happened? I was about to call you. You were taking so long." Jemma looked worried.

"No, it was nothing like that. Though I did take my time to give you two some privacy," Marcy reminded her.

Jemma laughed. "Yes, well, thank you for that. But do tell! What happened at the store?"

"You are not going to believe it, but I was hit on by the most handsome man. Looking like this no less." Marcy drew Jemma's attention to the blue t-shirt she wore and her oldest, most comfortable pair of denims.

Jemma chuckled and propped open the door for Marcy with her butt, while Marcy maneuvered past her. "OMG, spill. Tell me everything. Leave out no detail, no matter how small."

Jemma radiated excitement. And Marcy had to admit she liked having a female friend to share things with. They had gotten a lot closer this past year.

"Okay, I will. He was something." Marcy described the man as they put away the groceries.

"Keep talking. I am going to make us some sandwiches for dinner. Angel will be home later. I'll wrap his up for him."

Marcy told Jemma everything. The feelings it evoked. The questions he asked. The way she reacted and how easy it had been. After their quick meal, they carried their conversation into the living room with a glass of wine.

"Look at you," Jemma observed. "You look like the Cheshire cat, or the cat that caught the canary."

"It's just, oh, I don't know. He was so nice. Handsome. Do you think Angel knows him?"

"He must. He hasn't mentioned any of the new recruits, but if he is coming here, he has to be one. Blake Levine, huh. I'll definitely ask him and find out anything I can for you."

"Okay, but don't make it obvious you are asking for me. I would be mortified." It felt good to laugh. She hadn't done it in a long time. Not really. Unless it had been with her kids.

"I'm excited for you."

"Hey, nothing happened. He didn't ask me out or anything."

"That's because he knew he would see you tomorrow. If I am a betting woman…and I am, he will be by your side all day tomorrow and ask you out before you leave."

"Oh, I doubt it, and even if he does ask me for a date, I don't know if I should. I mean, my divorce isn't final. The kids…"

"Oh, phooey. Troy lives with another woman and you said the boys seem fine with it. It's not like you will move in with the man next week."

"Well, I need to be upfront with him tomorrow. I don't want to lead him on."

"You won't. That's not who you are. Be honest. Be yourself."

"I guess I am still a little bit in shock that such a good-looking man was flirting with me. He probably didn't notice my rolls with this baggy t-shirt."

Jemma was not having that from her friend. She was always pointing out what she perceived to be her flaws, and if Jemma knew her friend as well as she did and what she had gone through the past year, she suspected those insecurities came from Troy. Marcy just repeated what her ass of a soon-to-be ex said to her over the years. "Marcy, you really have to stop putting yourself down. You're a beautiful woman. I have always thought so. You have those high cheekbones, the perfect nose. Your skin is like porcelain even in Texas. You have gorgeous, wavy chestnut hair that never gets frizzy. And your green eyes have these little flecks of gold. And as for your body, well, woman, you're like me. You've got a curvy figure that will attract any guy. And you don't have rolls. You had twins and you have a little extra skin. Wear that with pride, woman. You have bounced back like no woman I have ever known who has a kid."

Marcy looked down at her midsection. "I have twenty pounds to lose."

"Who says that? Troy? That's bullshit. You are perfect just the way you are."

Marcy didn't have a reply. She wasn't used to someone complimenting her. Her boys always told her she was pretty, but they loved her. They had to say that, didn't they?

"Hi, honey, I'm home," came the rumble of Angel's voice. "Hey, girls," he added as he came into the living room.

"Hi, honey. I made you a sandwich. It's in the refrigerator."

"Thanks, babe. I'm starved. Hi, Marcy. I'm going to eat, then show you how to operate the security system. I need you to download the app, though, onto your phone."

"I left my phone on the kitchen table."

"I can do it for you. What's the passcode?"

Marcy told him. He went back into the kitchen and came back with his sandwich and her phone. He popped a squat on the floor and worked her phone with one hand while he ate his sandwich with the other.

"So, how did the shopping go? Get everything you need?" Angel asked.

Jemma gazed over Angel's head at her friend Marcy. "Oh, yes. She got everything she needed."

Marcy laughed at the expression on her friend's face. She definitely got something extra at the store. Angel remained oblivious while he installed the app.

He handed her the phone. "Check it out."

Marcy saw four grainy, moving images showing her the entrance to the ranch, the front of her house, the back of the house, and the area around the barn. The images rotated on the screen. "This is so cool."

"It sure is. I set it so you get a notification anytime something crosses one of the sensors or hidden cameras. Mostly you will see animals, but it is good to have. Before you get out of the car, tap the app, and check for any alerts." He pointed to an icon on the screen. "If you see something red, it means the cameras caught an image of movement. Tap it. Then you can go back and review any movement on the property for the whole day in just a few seconds prior to getting out of the vehicle. It will store images of movement and you just slide the images over like a slideshow."

"This is perfect, Angel. Thank you. It will definitely give me peace of mind."

"Me, too. Both of us will sleep easier knowing it's there. Hey, I'm going to grab a beer. You ladies want me to top off your wine glasses?" Angel asked, getting up from his position on the floor in front of Jemma.

"Yes, please," Jemma replied and smiled when he swiftly planted a kiss on top of her head.

Marcy knew Angel and Jemma were perfect together. Love shone through every action and every exchange between them. She had loved her husband in the beginning, but she now recognized it was not this type of love. One that was selfless and full of care and concern for the other person. Her husband had been a selfish man from the beginning, but she had over-looked it because he had been so handsome and so focused on building his career. In her late teens and early twenties, the idea of marrying someone who was going to be a doctor overshadowed all of his flaws.

She was mature enough to recognize that now. She loved the boys they shared together but couldn't help envy the type of love and relationship that Jemma and Angel shared. It's true they were newlyweds, but they had been this way even before their marriage. From the beginning of their relationship, Jemma had sparkled.

Marcy wanted that kind of love.

CHAPTER 12

Jemma had been right. Blake came straight to greet her when he arrived. "Marcy, you look nice today. It's good to see you again."

"Thank you, Blake." Marcy made the introductions to Jemma and Angel. Behind his back, Jemma threw her a thumbs up sign. And throughout the day, as he circulated and introduced himself to other people, he always came back around to Marcy for small talk. When he wasn't near, she found her eyes searching for him. Angel and some of the others had challenged him to a game of horseshoes. He fit right in with the old and new members of the TVFD.

"I like him, Marcy," Angel told her in passing to go man the grills. His comment made her wonder what Jemma had told him last night after they had gone to bed.

When Blake was off playing cornhole with some of the kids from Pop's ranch, Jemma cornered her. "So, he's divorced, ten years ago. Single. Detective from

New York. No kids. Parents retired in Arizona. Loves sports. No siblings. Cousins in New York."

"Damn, girl, you work fast," Marcy teased her friend. "Where did you get all that information?"

"Here and there. Listening in. Some from Elena and some from Jennifer. She is Deputy Logan's sister. He works out of Banderas like Blake."

"Oh." Though Blake had come to her several times as he made the rounds they really hadn't gotten to talk much. He was now tossing a football with Jimmy Peterson and Bailey Reynolds, two high school boys whose fathers were both TVFD.

"Okay, gotta run. Food is out, so go grab a plate and help yourself," Jemma said, running into the house to get more paper plates.

Marcy went to stand in line with the others, and when she felt someone behind her, she turned to greet him or her in the line. She found herself looking up into Blake's gorgeous brown eyes.

"Having fun?" he asked.

"Yes. Wish my kids were here, though. They would have had a lot of fun today."

"You mentioned they were at your ex's for the weekend."

"Yes, well, soon-to-be-ex," she confessed. When his eyes clouded over, she added, "We've been separated nearly eight months. Marriage was over long before that. He has a new girlfriend. But he's fighting me on some of the terms of the divorce."

"Ouch, sorry about that. My divorce went smoothly.

We both wanted it and didn't have anything worth fighting over."

"Yes, it does get more complicated when you have property and children," she admitted.

"Mind if join you for dinner? I've been wanting to spend time with you all day, and we haven't had more than a few minutes here and there. I had to meet my fellow volunteers and their families."

Marcy laughed. "Yes, there sure is a lot of them, but they also have plenty of these get-togethers, so you'll get to know them in no time. It's like an extended family if you ask Jemma and Angel. Be prepared."

"That's nice, though. You've always got somewhere to go and good people to be with." They had both reached the table laden with food. They began to fill their plates. "I don't have a large family so it'll be cool to be part of this one."

"Very," Marcy assured him. She told him how the whole community and surrounding area helped to clean up within a few months of the devastating tornado that had swept through Tarpley.

"That's fantastic. Yes, I see some of the damage around, but nothing of what it must have been like right after."

Marcy told him more about the storm. "Luckily, none of the tornados hit my house in Medina, or Angel's place in Banderas where I live now. I am renting from him."

"You have any family in the area that got hit?" he asked, wanting to know more about Marcy.

"No. My parents and my sister and her family live

in San Antonio. My ex brought us out here for a job. I love the area, though."

"You don't plan to move back there after the divorce?"

"Nope. I love this county and these small towns. I teach in Medina, but many of my kids live here, in Tarpley, Banderas, Medina, and the surrounding towns. My children's friends are here. They're starting high school this year and very excited about it. I don't want to pull them away from that. Plus, San Antonio isn't that far. I see my folks and sister quite a bit."

"That's nice."

They found a spot at one of the picnic tables some of the TVFD guys had dropped off earlier in the day. As they talked over their meal, she found Blake to be easy-going. He told her everything Jemma had mentioned, and she found herself revealing things to him as well. Things about her job and teaching, her kids, her love of horseback riding, and how she was getting dogs for the boys the following week. She also confessed how she wanted to write a book, the great American novel. He surprised her when he encouraged her to do it.

"I've always wanted to coach," he shared. He loved sports, baseball, football, and fishing.

"You'd get along great with my sons, Austin and Adam. They live, breathe, and sleep baseball. And if you want to coach, well, there are plenty of little leagues out there desperate for coaches."

"I'll definitely look into it."

Blake took her plate and carried it to the trash cans

70

when they finished eating. Angel had placed several around the property. "Care for a stroll?" he asked, offering Marcy his hand.

Without hesitation, Marcy took Blake's hand. He led her away from the gathering, and they strolled along the creek following its meandering path. When they had gone a sufficient distance, Blake stopped and turned to her. "Marcy, I like you. I think you like me. I'd love to take you out sometime, get to know you better. Would you say yes, if I asked?"

"I would." Her answer came tumbling out of her mouth before she could stop herself.

"Good," he replied. "I have also been wanting to do this." He tugged her hands to pull her close.

Marcy hadn't seen this coming but knew Blake was going to kiss her when his head bent to hers. She didn't feel fear like she thought she would when she imagined this moment but only reacted by turning up to him and meeting his lips with her own.

And, damn, if he wasn't good. He started slow, then sought more. She soon found her mouth parted for his seeking tongue. She didn't think of anything at all except for pleasure coursing through her body from his kiss, until she felt a dull ache at the back of her head where his fingers were wound into her hair. She pulled back in shock and his eyes cleared.

"What's wrong?" he asked, concerned. "Too fast. Do I need to slow down?" He knew she was just getting out of a long relationship, and he didn't want to scare her off, make her skittish. He could slow down if that was what she needed.

Marcy sighed, though she appreciated him asking. "Yes, er, no, it was nice. I liked it. I just didn't realize you had put your hands into my hair…"

"Your hair is gorgeous. I couldn't resist."

"Thank you." She blushed in the growing dusk. "I hurt my head the other night and have some stitches…" She broke off and reached for the back of her head where it was still tender. "You didn't feel the lump back there, did you?" she teased.

"Oh, shit, no. I didn't. I'm sorry," he quickly apologized. He had just forgotten about her incident in the moment.

When Marcy explained about the burglary, Blake told her he heard about it from some of the guys down at the station. They had discussed her case. He had only put two and two together later.

"Yes, it was horrible," Marcy confessed after he gave his condolences once more. She also explained Angel had insisted on getting a security system and again mentioned the new pups.

Blake was relieved to hear that Angel had taken some good precautions to prevent her from being attacked again on the property.

To pull them from the awkward moment, Marcy grabbed his hand, and they began to amble back to the party. It was time she headed home, anyway. Troy would be dropping off the boys at her place in a few hours, and Jemma or Angel had promised to sneak away from the celebration to take her home, she told him.

"Hey, I know they're still pretty busy here and must

be exhausted. I'm headed to Banderas. I don't mind giving you a lift after we help clean up, if you don't mind. It'll save them from having to go out there."

Her friends had done so much for her this weekend. Marcy smiled. "I'd like that." Plus, she'd get to spend more time with the handsome Blake Levine.

CHAPTER 13

On the ride home, Marcy and Blake chatted amicably. He asked her to explain more about her new security system. Touched by his interest in her safety, she showed him the app on her phone, and though he pronounced it was a good system, he still insisted on walking her to her door. Marcy felt the butterflies begin to swarm as he helped her out of his vehicle and took her hand in his as he led her up the few steps onto the wrap-around porch. When she turned to him after reaching her door, he was there. Tall, handsome, strong, and so darn appealing, she felt like a teenager all over again.

She knew when he bent to her what was going to happen next. A kiss. Unlike the earlier ones, this one was sweet and tender, but underneath she sensed the restrained passion. She was breathless when he ended it, and even a tad wobbly on her feet. His arm steadied her as she reached for the door.

"I had a lot of fun today, Marcy. I can't wait to see

you again." She saw the fire in his eyes. The kiss had done something to him as well.

She smiled shyly, still feeling the aftershocks of that kiss. "I had a great time, too. And yes, I can't wait to see you again, too."

Blake stepped back from her and nodded as he reluctantly turned around.

Marcy watched him as he went to his vehicle. "I'll call soon," he promised as he climbed back into his vehicle.

Marcy felt a flush in her cheeks, but took one deep breath before she turned the knob and headed inside. She was sure her friend Jemma would call her later and ask for details. But Marcy needed time to process it all. The last thing she had ever expected was to jump into a relationship yet here she was, doing exactly that. And the feelings Blake invoked in her, oh lord, she didn't know what she was getting herself into.

* * *

The next few days flew by for Marcy. School started the following week and the boys were home, enjoying all that the ranch had to offer. They had gotten chickens from a local rancher the previous day and put them inside the coop Angel had built on the property. The boys loved feeding them and checking on them each morning.

But today the boys were excited beyond measure.

"I can't believe we are actually getting dogs. Not

one, but two!" Adam shoveled the eggs Marcy had made into his mouth.

"Chocolate labs! They get pretty big, I think." Austin was refilling his plate. He stabbed two more sausages and another heaping pile of scrambled eggs. The boys ate like maniacs.

"You are each responsible for one of the dogs. Feeding them, walking them, training them," Marcy reminded them. She took a sip of her steaming cup of coffee. Her second already. She was going to need it to keep the boys calm until Angel arrived.

"Of course, Mom. We got this." Adam tapped his chest to reassure her. Marcy smiled. They were good boys and helped her out when she asked. She would have to remind them, until it became routine, she knew that, but the boys had wanted dogs for years. Troy had never wanted dogs in town. He hadn't wanted to fence in the property for a large breed and was absolutely against little dogs.

After breakfast the boys went to feed the chickens and play catch with one another until Angel arrived. Marcy checked her watch. It wouldn't be too long now. He had called her early this morning to tell her he would be over as soon as he picked up the twelve-week-old pups. She busied herself with the breakfast dishes and then joined the boys outside. As she sipped her now cold coffee while she watched the boys play, her phone rang. When she recognized Troy's number, she reluctantly accepted the call.

"The boys texted me." He started right away after she greeted him. "They said you got them dogs."

"Yes, I did. They will be arriving shortly." Marcy wanted to keep the conversation as brief as possible.

"That's great. They sounded excited. You know they can't bring them to my condo. They don't allow them."

"Of course, I understand." She saw the boys glance her way.

"Is it Angel? Is he running late?" Adam asked.

Marcy shook her head. "No. It's your dad. Just checking in."

"Oh, okay." Adam threw the ball to his brother who caught it without mishap.

Marcy lowered her voice so only Troy could hear her. She hated having arguments with their father in front of the boys. "No need to worry. This ranch is huge, and it's good to have them out here." She hesitated. "Troy, I, um, am glad you called, actually. I have been wanting to tell you something." She hadn't told him yet about the burglary. She hadn't wanted to do it in front of the boys when he had dropped them off last week. She got up and went inside. She watched the boys continue to play while she told Troy about the burglary attempt and getting hit on the head. "I got some stitches, but they are healing nicely."

"Marcy! Why didn't you call me when it happened?" He sounded genuinely upset.

"I didn't think you'd…"

"Don't say it, Marcy. Just because I fell out of love with you doesn't mean I don't care. You're still the mother of my children."

"Sorry, Troy. I guess that wasn't fair. But I didn't

want to worry the children about it and the last time I saw you they were both present."

"You could have called." How quickly his mood changed. Now he sounded cold and distant.

"I was going to tell you. I just had a lot to do. I installed a new security system here at the ranch, and well, that's another reason why I decided to get the boys the dogs they have always wanted. I am sure they will be the first to sound the alarm when there are strangers or new people on the property."

She heard him clear his voice and knew he was choosing his words carefully. "It is a good idea to have dogs on the ranch. Out there, dogs work. But I still wish you would have called me. I will check your stitches when I pick up the boys next weekend," Troy said.

"That's not necessary," Marcy assured him.

"It's not, but I am a surgeon. Which ER did you go to?"

"The one here in Banderas."

"When do they come out? The stitches?" he asked, then quickly added, "Do you need me to watch the kids when you go to the doctor?"

"No, I've made arrangements to have the doctor take them out on Monday right after my last class. The boys will be at baseball conditioning and I'll have time to get back to the high school before they get through."

"Okay, but if you need me to, I can pick them up and take them to dinner until your appointment is done."

"Thanks, Troy." It was nice of him to offer, she thought wryly.

After Marcy hung up with her soon-to-be-ex, she went back outside to wait with the boys. She had been surprised at how well that conversation had gone. She had thought about not telling him at all, but then thought better of it. With a divorce on the horizon, she felt it best to be upfront. She didn't want him using any information she held back against her if he really did fight for custody. They had two more required mediation meetings to attend before they took their case before a judge. She hoped it didn't come to that, but just in case, she had to be completely forthcoming. She wouldn't risk losing her boys.

Adam and Austin were fourteen years old, and they had been the center of her world since the day they were born. She was glad they weren't typical teenage boys who wanted to spend all of their time playing video games. They loved going outdoors and playing sports. They were above average students, and she was fine with that, though it had bothered her ex-husband that they weren't straight A students through middle school. But as a teacher, she knew better. It wasn't all about the grades. Yes, they were important, and more so in high school, but being well-rounded counted for a lot.

Both Austin and Adam were excited about starting high school, and though she had asked, they claimed they weren't embarrassed to be going to the same school where their mother taught. In fact, they were looking forward to it.

Moving to the ranch, despite the previous week's incident, had been a good thing for her and them. She needed a fresh start. She wouldn't miss the functions she had been forced to attend with her husband at the hospital. He was always trying to impress the hospital board members as he climbed the social ladder. His new Barbie doll of a girlfriend could take over those duties. She hated being so petty when it came to Nancy. But she just couldn't help herself. Something about the woman rubbed her the wrong way.

Marcy heard the new screen door open with a resounding *thwack*. Adam carried two water bottles and handed one to his brother, "I can't believe you're going to get us two dogs, Mom." Adam was still on a high from the news she had given them a few hours earlier. "Dad never wanted us to have them in the house."

"But this is different," Austin defended his father. "This is a ranch, and dogs need to be able to run and play, and they'll have plenty of room here."

"That's true, Austin. Your dad is glad I'm getting them for you now that we live here. Having these kinds of dogs, well, they really need the space," Marcy agreed.

"You said Labradors. I know they are a medium to large size, but I don't know how big they actually get. Do you, Mom?" Adam asked.

"You know, I'm not quite sure, but we can probably get a book about that breed at the bookstore."

"That'd be great," Austin replied. "Now, that would be something I would want to read."

Marcy laughed. Her boys read when they *had* to.

That was one thing they did not have in common with her, her love of books. Marcy glanced at her watch and knew Angel would arrive soon.

She sat in the rocker, while both boys sat on the porch, letting their legs hang off the side sipping their bottles of water.

Austin's head picked up. "Hey, I think he's coming." He pointed toward the road. Both boys hopped off the porch and Marcy stood. She saw the tell-tale plume of dust rise in the air that meant a vehicle was coming. She smiled and walked down the three steps to join her twin sons in the area in front of the house where cars parked.

"Man, Angel is awesome for getting us these dogs," Austin said. Marcy resisted the urge to ruffle her son's hair. At his age, he would not appreciate it.

Adam added, "He is great. He said I can do my volunteer hours for high school at his clinic. I think I'd like to be a veterinarian and work with animals like him. He and Jemma are great together, too, don't you think, Mom?"

The boys had known Jemma for a long time, but Angel was new to them. "He is a wonderful man, and Jemma and he love each other, that's for sure."

"Dad liked the idea of me being a vet. I'll be a doctor, too, just for animals instead of humans."

Austin piped in, "But he didn't like my idea of being a deputy or a sheriff. I want to be like Jack Riggs when I grow up. He is the coolest. With that Stetson hat and the vehicle he drives and saving all those people."

"Sheriff Riggs is one of the good ones," Marcy

confirmed, thinking of another law enforcement man, whom she thought was one of the good ones, too, though it might be premature to say for certain. He had texted her early that morning asking if she was up and could take a call. He apologized for not calling sooner, but he had been out of town working a cold case in San Antonio. He then asked to take her out that weekend. She said yes. She was looking forward to it.

When Angel's truck pulled up in front of the house and he opened the door, two twelve-week-old chocolate Labradors bounded out of the truck and ran straight for the boys like they knew who they were. Marcy's smile widened seeing the dogs lick her boys' hands and faces, then flip over for belly rubs in the dirt. The boys laughed at the dogs' antics.

"This one with the white foot is mine," called Adam, staking his claim. Though it was clear the dog claimed him first. The dog tilted its head to the side, while he scratched the puppy under the chin.

"They are twins, like us," Austin said. "The only difference is yours has that bit of white on its foot."

"Thank you, Angel," first one boy, then the other chimed in, "Yes, thank you. These are the best dogs. They love to play."

"They sure do, boys, and they need you to play with them hard every day for a while at least. They are going to be missing their momma, and you need to get them nice and tired each day so they sleep good."

"Yes, sir."

"We will," promised Austin.

"Thank you, Angel," Marcy repeated her children's gratitude.

"Not at all. I've got a box in the car with some of the stuff you will need."

"You didn't have to do that."

"I'm a vet. I got a lot of this stuff lying around. Let me get it." From the back of the pickup Angel pulled down a large box and brought it over to Marcy. He set it on the ground in front of her. Inside, she saw dog bowls and chew toys, puppy food, and blankets, as well as an assortment of other odds and ends she had planned to shop for later that day. "The blankets have their momma's scent on them. Keep those where they sleep at night."

"Angel, really, this is too much."

He pushed her thanks aside with a wave of his hand. Angel continued to give them simple directions for the puppies' care the first few weeks and explained how to train the dogs if they were going to be kept inside.

"Yes, sir. We can do all of that," Adam said.

"But they need to be kept in the barn during the day while we are at school. I don't need my furniture all torn up," Marcy reminded them.

"Aren't they going to be lonely there all day?" asked Adam.

"Nope. Not at all. They have each other, and they were born and lived in the barn at the Peterson place. It is what they are used to," Angel assured them. "Oh, Marcy, just remember they'll need their next round of shots in four weeks. So, in a month give me a call, and I can swing by or you can bring them to me."

"Gotcha." Marcy gave him the thumbs up sign.

"So, guys what are you gonna name these little beasts?" Angel asked.

Adam looked up in surprise. "What? We get to name them? They don't already have one?"

"Yes, sirree. You get to name them. The Petersons didn't name them yet. They're both boys."

"Well, I'm gonna call mine Chewie because look at him," Adam declared. He was chewing something between his toes. Marcy laughed at the dog's unusual position and how frantically he was working at his paw.

"What about you, Austin? What are you gonna name yours?" Angel asked.

"That's pressure, man." Austin's hand went straight for his hair like it always did when he was nervous or thinking hard. The unnamed dog jumped up on Austin and stretched. Austin gazed down into the brown eyes of the dog and Marcy's heart melted. It was like love at first sight. "His name is Champ. It kind of goes along with Chewie."

"Those are great names," Marcy said, trying to keep the tears from springing to her eyes. "Chewie and Champ Fields, welcome to the family." Marcy knelt down between her children and the dogs approached her while she gave them appreciative scratches on their head and behind their ears.

"Hey, guys." Angel pulled a chewed-up frisbee out of the box. "They love to play catch, so why don't you guys take them over to the fenced-in grassy area over there and play with them for a bit. You should also keep them leashed so they don't run off until they know this is their home. Unleash them from now on when they are in the house, barn, or in that area over there." He quickly snapped a short leash onto each, and the dogs tugged at the foreign feeling.

"I don't think Chewie likes it," Adam said of the leash.

"He probably doesn't. But at least a few months while outside, okay? Once you start a routine and feed them, then they know where they get their dinner and love, and they won't run off. But until then, you need to keep them close."

"Okay. We promise," Adam replied, taking the frisbee from Angel and pulling his dog after him until Chewie figured out what Adam wanted him to do.

Once the boys were off, Angel said, "I can microchip them if you want when they come in for their shots in a month."

"Yes, I think so, the boys would be heartbroken if they got lost."

"Get them nice and tired," Angel called out to the boys who had already unleashed the dogs inside the fenced-in area which Angel had built last year for the dogs he treated. It was the perfect setup for the two new puppies until they got the lay of the land. "You want them to sleep tonight and not keep you up. They're gonna be sad little dudes for a while without their momma."

"Well, they can have our momma because she's the

best momma in the world," Adam yelled from across the yard. "Thanks for letting us get these dogs, Mom."

"Yeah, thanks, Mom."

Tears came. "You're both welcome," Marcy called back.

The day had been a good one. Tomorrow would be even brighter. She would get to see Blake again.

CHAPTER 14

Marcy heard Angel out in the living room with the boys playing a video game, and she listened to their competitive chatter. The dogs, Chewie and Champ, were taking one of their puppy naps on the huge pillow the boys had purchased together the day before for them. The trip to Pet Smart had been a huge success. The boys had wanted to pick out a few things for their dogs, and after calling their dad to tell him the news, Troy had put a hundred dollars into each of their accounts so they could buy what they wanted for the puppies. Marcy had to admit he was being much nicer about the dogs than she had thought he would be. Though he did tell the boys the dogs would not be allowed in his condo.

Jemma was in the bedroom with Marcy helping her to get ready for her date. Blake had called her earlier in the evening to tell her that he was going to take her out to dinner, then if she felt up for it, he had heard of a place called Boots in Banderas that was fun. She knew about the place but had never been as her ex-husband didn't particularly care for country line dancing. She had always loved country music and to dance. She had readily agreed to the idea.

She had enjoyed the day with the boys, the shopping trip, and dogs, but all day, her stomach felt queasy. Her doubts weren't about Blake, but about going out with someone at all. She was not sure she was doing the right thing. She was technically still married, though separated for quite some time. And her husband was already living with another woman. But she also worried her boys wouldn't like it. As she tried on clothes for her date, Marcy thought about the conversation she'd had earlier with the twins concerning Blake.

She had fretted about telling them all morning, then over lunch before the trip to Pet Smart, she broke the news. At first, they had looked at her dumbfounded. Clearly, they had been shocked to hear the news. But Adam was the first to recover which was typical.

"I think it's great, Mom." His initial shock passed, and he went back to his usual chipper demeanor and continued to wolf down the turkey sandwich and potato chips she had prepared for lunch. As an afterthought, his mouth full of potato chips, he added, "You deserve to find someone who treats you nice." Then, he elbowed his brother.

Marcy looked at Austin who wasn't smiling or eating. He remained mute, but eventually looked up and made eye contact. He shrugged his shoulders. "I guess, I'm okay with it." Austin was always the more sensitive one, so she reached over and patted his hand. He turned his over and gave her hand a gentle squeeze.

"Hey, no leaving me out of this!" Adam exclaimed and reached for Marcy's other hand. She gave both boys' hands a squeeze and laughed.

"Well, it's just a first date. His name is Blake Levine. He's a deputy and works for Riggs." She noticed at the mention of Riggs' name, whom Austin greatly respected, he sat up a little straighter and didn't look so sullen. "I met him at Jemma and Angel's barbecue. Oh, wait, I actually met him the day before at the grocery store," she self-corrected.

"Look at Mom," Adam teased. "Picking out guys with the produce."

Austin laughed. So did Marcy. She loved how Adam could always turn the mood around for his brother. "Now, stop teasing me. I am nervous enough as it is."

"Okay, but let's get going. I am anxious to take these puppies to the store and let them pick out some of their own toys."

Marcy saluted her sons. "Let's get this show on the road."

"Here," Jemma said, handing Marcy yet another blouse from her closet and interrupting her train of thought. "This one. Definitely this one. Take that one off," she ordered. "This one will show off your assets if you know what I mean." Jemma shook what her momma gave her and Marcy laughed. She accepted the lavender blouse with the V-neck. It was one of her favorites. It shimmered and flared slightly at her hips. She pulled it over her head.

"You should tuck it into your jeans. This way you can show off your hips."

Marcy disagreed. "I like how it shapes me."

"It's perfect," Jemma pronounced and looked through Marcy's jewelry box. "Damn, girl, you have some nice things in here."

She did. Troy had given her jewelry for every birthday and holiday. But she only wore them at his work functions.

Marcy slid into one of her designer pair of jeans. She happily noticed they went on easily. Last time she had tried them on, they had been a tad snug. Living on the ranch, she was much more active and noticed her clothes fit her better than usual. She didn't dare get on a scale, though. The scale had never been her friend. "Troy was generous with me in the beginning. Most of those pieces are from him, though some are from my parents. The stuff Troy gave me I want to save for the boys when they have wives and daughters to give them to."

"Well, with that neckline, I don't suggest anything too fancy. How about this necklace and these earrings?"

Marcy examined Jemma's selections and declared they were perfect.

The earrings were a simple set of diamond studs her parents had given her as a college graduation gift. And the gold chain with the small heart-shaped medallion that said 'Best Mom Ever' was a gift from her sons on Mother's Day. They had saved up their allowance and chipped in to buy it for her.

Marcy turned to her makeup while Jemma made herself comfortable on the bed. "I'm so excited for you, Marcy. You're going to have a great time."

"I hope so. He's really nice. But, if truth be told, I still feel weird about going out when my divorce isn't final."

She heard Jemma sigh. "I get that, but don't think about the long term. It's just one date. This is good. It will help you build up your confidence and get that first awkward post-divorce date out of the way."

Marcy chuckled. "Well, since you put it that way." Jemma laughed with her just as there was a soft knock on the door, and the dogs went wild being woken up from their nap.

By the time Marcy came from her room, with Jemma behind her, the dogs had quieted down and were wagging their tails, greeting their new guest.

When Blake stood up to greet her, he took her breath away. Troy had been a good-looking man, but Blake, well, he just oozed manhood. It was his size, and the way he carried himself. He was large, and his muscles rippled under his black dress shirt. The jeans he paired with it fit him like a glove.

"Marcy, you look beautiful." He stared at her.

She blushed and thanked him. "You look nice, Blake. You remember Angel and Jemma, and these are my boys, Adam and Austin, and their new dogs, Chewie and Champ."

"Hi, everyone. Yes, nice to see you guys again, Angel." He shook his hand and nodded in Jemma's direction. Then he turned to her sons and held out his hand. "It's nice to meet you both. Your mom told me you like baseball."

"Yes, sir," both replied, using their manners and being polite.

Blake must have glanced at the screen behind them. "Oh, man, you guys are playing Rainbow Six. I love that game!"

"You play?" Austin asked, one eyebrow raised.

"I most certainly do."

"Cool. We have to take turns playing against Angel. But maybe you could play with us sometime and we could do teams."

"Sure, I'd love to do that. You guys play online?"

"Sure do. But only on the weekends." They looked behind them at Marcy.

"Fair enough. I am Ghostrecon38. Look me up. I'd love to have a match with you guys."

"Awesome."

"Sweet."

"I got Adam, and you two are going down!" Angel declared using two fingers to point at Austin and Blake. Everyone laughed.

"Okay, well, you guys have fun tonight," Jemma said from the rear of the group, helping to usher Marcy and Blake on their way.

"Yes, have fun, Mom," Adam and Austin called simultaneously.

"Thanks, boys. Have fun with Angel and Jemma."

* * *

The restaurant they went to in Banderas wasn't overly fancy. It was called the Steak Joint, and Marcy had eaten there before. A hostess sat them in a booth in the back and gave them some privacy. "The food is great here, Blake. You'll like it. They have fantastic prime rib, and the porterhouse is melt in your mouth delicious."

"Logan, er, Deputy Logan, told me this was the best place in town."

"It is." Marcy agreed. "You won't be disappointed."

His smile was playful when he came back with a quick retort. "How can I be when I am here with you?"

She laughed. "Flattery will get you everywhere," she teased, then blushed when his eyes went round. "I mean, um…"

He laughed. "No worries. I understand."

Marcy fanned her flaming cheeks with her napkin. "I haven't been on a date in a long time. I guess I am out of practice."

"Same, actually. And you are doing fine. I promise."

When the waiter came to drop off their beers, he took the rest of their order. Both Marcy and Blake ordered the prime rib with a loaded baked potato and a salad as an appetizer. After her initial faux-pas she found conversation with Blake easy and pleasant. Not only was he a great listener when she answered his questions about her job and kids, but he also kept her entertained with stories of his childhood in New York and his antics with his cousin who lived down the block from him.

Sadly, both of his cousin's parents had been killed an automobile accident when he was just eighteen. Though he wasn't his brother, he was like one to Blake and his two daughters were like nieces to him.

"That's nice that you are close to him," Marcy commented as she took a bite of her baked potato.

"We grew up together, and after his folks passed, he lived with us while going to college. I went into the military, then when I got out, I attended the police academy. He went to law school."

"My sister Lena's husband is an attorney. Corporate law."

"My cousin is an assistant district attorney now. His interest was always criminal law. He likes prosecuting criminals."

"Guess that runs in the family."

"It does. I catch them and he puts them away." He talked about his father who also had been a detective.

She told him about her sister and her nieces and her parents. Marcy was delighted he took an interest in her stories of the students and the curriculum she taught. She was surprised to learn he was an avid reader, but because of his work and his hours, he often did not get to enjoy reading as much as he liked. He'd read the most recent Grisham novel, and they talked about it. They both loved procedurals and stories about crime and the law.

"Yes, I love crime books. But I really love young adult fiction. There is so much kids can learn about life from books."

"I agree. I loved *The Giver* when I was in school. It was one of my favorites."

"Mine, too. I would love to write a book someday. In fact, I have a really good idea for one and I think I may try to get it down on paper."

"Absolutely. It's never too late to chase a dream." Marcy beamed at him. He was so friggin' amazing. Troy had thought her pursuing writing was a silly waste of time. "So, what is it going to be about?" he asked.

"It is going to be a travel log, a story about an aunt and her niece who go on a summer spree together. They are going to get into all kinds of crazy situations, while her aunt drives all over the country for her work. The aunt's sister wanted her to take her daughter for the summer to get away from a bad crowd she was getting involved with. As they travel, we will learn more about the aunt's life, the niece's experiences, and the two will learn from each other. The story will change both of their lives for the better."

"It really does sound amazing. I bet you will use some of your experiences with your own students in it."

"Yes!" Marcy declared, ecstatic he had guessed her motives.

"Always the teacher. You're wanting to impart all the lessons that helped your students over the years."

"Yes, that and more," Marcy added. "Some of the stories I've heard from other teachers, too. Our kids have taught us about life just as much as, if not more, than they learn from us."

"I guess that's why I want to coach, too. I think it's important for kids, boys especially, to have a strong male role model to look up to. Thought I'd be that for my own kids someday. I have always wanted to be a father. But after my first marriage failed, I didn't want to go that route for a while. I'm getting close to forty, thirty-eight by the way, and I think I'm ready again."

Marcy took the hint. He wanted a family. She didn't know if she wanted to have more kids. But Jemma's voice in her head told her to hush up. It was just a first date. Enjoy it. It's practice. "I'm thirty-six," she told him. There was a momentarily lapse in the conversation, and she worried Blake might think she was too old to bear more children.

"Yes, I have tried dating someone younger. Not purposefully. I discovered I have nothing in common with a woman who is more than ten years younger. When I mention a past President, and the girl doesn't know who the heck I'm talking about, well, that's just a deal breaker." He laughed.

Marcy laughed with him. His words, though humorous, also helped to build her confidence. Blake appeared to be a good man, incredibly handsome, and she was sure women threw themselves at him all the time. Yet he had chosen her to ask out at the barbecue. "I can name all of them," she teased.

He ordered them each another drink. "So, you had your kids right out of college?" he asked.

"Yes, that was the plan. Troy wanted to have kids while we were young and could enjoy them, but he was so busy first with med school, and then with building his practice, he missed a lot of the twins' childhood."

"Are the kids close with their father?"

"Yes, actually. Thankfully. They don't have much in common, but he goes to all the important events. He isn't into sports like they are, but he does like hiking and skiing, and the boys enjoy doing those things with him."

"That's good. I've seen way too many young men in the system, and a lot of them, and I mean a lot, were there because they didn't have that strong male role model to look up to. And even in divorce, it's good to see he takes an active role."

Marcy nodded. "Yes, as much as Troy and I disagreed, his faults were mostly in the life partner area, not with the kids. We are fortunate the kids understand, or seem to so far, that we are better apart than together."

Blake cleared his throat before speaking. "May I ask why you and Troy are getting divorced? I don't mean to pry, and if you don't feel comfortable talking about it, I understand."

"No, not at all. It's pretty common knowledge he is, and was, a philanderer. Well, common knowledge to everybody but me. I mean, I only caught him one time, and he told me it was over, but our relationship never really recovered after that. This happened when the boys were eight. Last Christmas, I made plans for a family getaway, and when he called to cancel, I drove straight to the hospital. I was so mad. But the staff told me he had taken the weekend off for a family trip. I checked his bank card and saw the hotel bills. I confronted him, and he confessed he was leaving me, had met someone else who was a better fit for him."

"I'm so sorry, Marcy. It's seriously his loss. You are a remarkable woman."

"Well, thank you for thinking so." She took a sip of her drink. "His new girlfriend is a thin blonde. She's gorgeous, at least ten years younger. She looks like a Barbie doll." Marcy let her last comment slip and wished she could take it back. "Her name is Nancy. The boys don't seem to mind her." She rambled but couldn't stop herself. "Anyway, he moved out of the house the following day. I heard through the grapevine, then, that Nancy hadn't been the first, but one of many women he had been with over the years. There had been nurses and other young female staff. All those times I thought he was working extra shifts, he apparently was not."

"Wow, I am sorry. It sucks. I went through a similar situation with my ex. We were both young. Only twenty-three. I was just out of the police academy and working crazy hours, plus studying for the detective's exam. Not making excuses for her, but she wanted to party and met someone else."

"Yes, it sucks," Marcy agreed.

After dinner they went to Boots. Blake surprised her by asking her to dance. And for a city boy, she was happily surprised at how good he was at line dancing to the country western music.

"Wow, Blake," she laughed as he spun her around. "You are a great dancer. You can kick with the best of them."

"Country kickin', huh?" he asked with one eyebrow arched in question, as he pulled her back into him after pulling her under his arm.

"Not exactly. In Texas we call it cowboy dancing, or kicker dancing."

Blake laughed. When the music changed to a ballad, he pulled her even closer. "Well, I don't care what they call it, but I like dancing close with you best of all."

Marcy blushed, and her heart beat rapidly. She could really get used to this. Blake was so kind, so good-natured. So damn sexy! Just thinking about him made her flush. She laid her head on his chest to hide her thoughts from him as if he could read her mind, swayed in time to the music, and enjoyed being in his arms.

When the song was over, she tilted her head to look up at him, and he was smiling down at her. She knew the look in his eyes. Knew he was going to kiss her. Again. She didn't shy away when he took her lips for the third time, but she wasn't counting. She hadn't planned on it. Feeling this good, finding someone, having fun. Her pull toward him was undeniable. It made her hope there would be more than kisses with Blake. Definitely. She hoped he felt whatever this was between them was something good. Because she was sure hoping this was something they could explore.

Toward midnight, Blake remarked, "Come on, I better get you home to your kids." He took her hand in his and led her to his car.

CHAPTER 15

The first day of school had gone off without a hitch. Marcy loved her schedule and her new students, especially those in her upper level creative writing classes. She had worked with them in previous years, and they had established quite the bond over their shared love of writing.

"This year, I really want to do something different with them. I want to bring in a lot of local authors to talk to them about different careers, the writing process, and publishing," Marcy mentioned to Calliope as they ate lunch.

"I might know someone," Callie replied, as she munched on some grapes in the teacher breakroom.

"Really? That would be awesome, Callie."

"I can't make any guarantees, but I do happen to know a really talented author, though he's kind of reclusive. I can promise to work on him for you."

"Thanks, I would really appreciate that."

Jemma then asked Callie how things were going

with Tank, and Callie said things were great, but then quickly switched gears and put Marcy in the spotlight. "So, how about you, Marcy? I heard through the proverbial grapevine you went out with a 'certain' new deputy in Banderas. Do tell?"

Marcy flashed Jemma a look. But Jemma just laughed and shrugged her shoulders. "Oopsy. Sorry. But you wouldn't tell me anything Friday night." Jemma feigned pouting.

"That's because Blake stayed for a bit afterwards. I offered him coffee and he accepted. I couldn't very well tell you about it while he was there." Marcy blushed profusely.

"But you didn't call all weekend," Jemma chastised.

"I had the kids and school to get ready for…" Marcy lamely replied, but the truth was she had needed time to process how wonderful their first date had been.

"So," Callie cut in, "what happened after Jemma and Angel left?"

"We talked. That's all. Well, he may or may not have kissed me again and we may or may not have made plans for Wednesday while the boys have baseball conditioning."

"Ooo." Jemma smiled, happy for her friend.

"But enough for now. I've gotta run," Marcy said, cutting off her friend when she saw the time and knew her next class was starting soon. "The bell is about to ring, I have one more class, and then need to get these darn stitches out while the boys are at baseball conditioning after school. I promise to fill you in later."

"Thank you! Now was that too much to ask for?" Jemma laughed as she turned toward her friend Callie.

"Have a great rest of your day, girls," Marcy called over her shoulder as she made her way out into the hall. For once, she was glad to escape the breakroom and her two friends. And it was only because her thoughts about Blake Levine were all over the place, and she couldn't even explain it to herself, let alone her friends.

* * *

The boys sat in the backseat together as she drove them home after baseball conditioning. They liked being with the high school kids and felt they would learn a lot by having the JV and Varsity teams in practice together. Marcy enjoyed listening to their banter. No, she was not disappointed in moving a bit further away from work. The car drive was thirty minutes, but it would get her the information she loved to hear. When, she asked them about their day, they, like typical teens, clammed up and said, "It was fine. Great. No homework." When the twins chatted with each other, she learned so much more. Though occasionally she dropped in a question of clarification or two.

"Man, I can't wait to get home. I'm starving."

"I'll start on dinner, but you boys need to get the pups out of the barn and feed them. Then walk them or play in the fenced-in area." The dogs had cried for their momma a few nights; because they were puppies and their sleeping patterns were not fixed yet, they did wake in the night and caused some mischief. The boys had been good about playing with them a couple of times a day to expend that energy. But with school having started, their routine was changing again.

"Got it, Mom," Adam replied. "After dinner, I have algebra homework. Can you believe it? First day of school!"

"Me, too," Austin groaned. He was good in math, but just hated homework. "I'll help you with it."

"Thanks." Adam always had a hard time with math. But the boys leaned on each other to help where the other was weaker. It was a blessing they held on to those twin bonds throughout middle school. Marcy had heard stories of twins who didn't stay close. She was glad her sons never seemed to argue or disagree for long and were always able to settle their issues quickly between each other.

As Marcy made a mental note to check their math homework later and figured out what she would make for dinner, settling on burritos, she noticed a dark blue pickup truck racing up behind her on the highway. Nothing was coming in the other direction. She pulled close to the edge of the road but maintained her speed in case the man in a rush wanted to pass her.

She peered ahead and the way was still clear, though she knew a turn was coming. The vehicle in her rearview mirror would be cutting it close, so she took her foot off the gas to slowly decelerate her car to give him a bit of extra time.

"Boys, you got your seatbelts on?" she asked.

"Yes."

"Of course."

They were good about that, but whenever Marcy got nervous with them in the car, she always asked. The truck was nearly upon them but not switching lanes. Marcy pulled over the white line to let him know he could pass. To her relief, the vehicle moved slightly over, then started to pass just as the road began to turn and the dotted line disappeared. Marcy glanced ahead and saw an oncoming car. She pressed the break into the turn, and at the same time noticed the blue pickup swerved back into her lane. He was going to hit her. She slammed on the breaks as much as she dared without sending them forward, but she felt the pain of the seatbelt cutting into her. The truck clipped her front end, and it sent her into a half spin. She hit the breaks even harder and saw one of the boys' bookbags fly into the front seat. She heard Austin cry out, "Oh, shit!"

Adam yelled something. The car finally stopped turning as she careened off the highway into the ditch on the side of the road, but thankfully it wasn't a deep one.

"Are you guys okay?" Marcy asked as she quickly removed her seatbelt. She knew she would have a bruise across her shoulder, but the seatbelt had saved her life. All of their lives. That asshole! The man in the blue truck had sped off without stopping. She wanted to curse a storm but resisted.

"I'm okay, Mom," Austin assured her, and Marcy turned in her seat to check both boys.

"I'm okay, too," Adam said, but she could tell he was shaken up a bit.

"Just scared the sh..." Austin stopped himself. He had slipped once and that was okay under the circumstances, but even in this moment, he was such a good boy he thought better of the words he used as she had taught them.

"Scared the shit out of me, too!" Marcy declared emphatically and both boys' mouths dropped open at her language. Then they laughed, the aftereffect of an adrenaline rush followed by relief they hadn't been seriously injured.

After a moment to regain herself, Marcy realized she needed to see if there had been any damage and if the car could be driven out of the ditch. "Stay in here," she told the boys as she cautiously opened the door.

As soon as she did, she saw the small wisp of smoke coming from underneath the hood. Then she noticed the front wheel. It looked bent underneath the right front quarter panel. Just great! She couldn't drive it in that condition. She would need to call a tow truck.

"Sorry, boys. We are going to need to call the highway patrol to report we have been in a hit and run accident, and then call for a tow truck. This may take a while."

"Darn it!"

"Oh, man!"

Yup. This was the last thing she needed right now.

* * *

It was late that evening when Marcy finally got the chance to call Jemma. "I'm glad you called the DPS and Officer Jones stayed with you until the tow truck came," Jemma said.

"Yes, me, too. Tank came to take the car to Otto Repairs. He is having someone drive over a loaner car until mine is fixed. I just can't believe it. I mean this is the last thing I needed right now. My credit card will be maxed out."

"Gosh, I am sorry to hear that."

"Thankfully, we get paid next week."

"Have you told Troy yet?"

"Yes. He called to ask about the boys' first day, and they mentioned it."

"You'd think he would offer to help out."

"No such luck. He did offer to drop the custody suit and give me the fifty thousand from our savings account, but he wants the cash from the sale of the house."

"What a jerk," Jemma said.

"Yeah, I just can't accept it. I deserve more."

"You definitely do. And what about Blake? Have you spoken to him today?"

"We have plans Wednesday. I didn't know if I should call him or not."

"Call him. It'll show him you are interested as much as he is."

Marcy thought about it. So far, he had always been the one to call. Maybe she should. She just didn't know what to say. The boys were in the Austin's room watching a movie, so after she hung up with Jemma, she called him.

He answered after the first ring. "Well, hello, beautiful. To what do I owe the pleasure?" Marcy imagined him smiling on the other end of the line. It gave her butterflies.

"Hi, Blake. I just wanted to say hello," she replied. Then added, "I'm looking forward to seeing you on Wednesday."

"Same. I ate at a little Tex-Mex place for lunch today near your high school. I thought it might be a good place to go since you have just a few hours."

"Rosa's Tex-Mex. Yes, it's good. I can pick up the boys something, too. They are always starving right after conditioning, then I won't need to cook."

"Speaking of the boys, how was their first day? And yours?"

Marcy told him about their day and the accident.

"Damn it! I hope Trooper Jones finds the bastard. I can't believe the driver didn't stop and offer assistance."

"Same here. I wish I got his license plate, but we were into the turn and I was focused on other things."

"I bet. I'm glad you're all okay." She told him about the bruise and the condition of the car. "Shit! I hate that you have to deal with this. You've had a real string of bad luck lately. First the burglary, now a hit and run!"

"I know. It's been a lot to deal with. Thankfully, Tank gave me a loaner from Otto Repairs."

"Yes, I met him the other day. Nice man. His girl is

Callie, right? He mentioned she worked over at the high school. You know her?"

"Yes, she's a good friend. Great teacher, too."

Adam and Austin came out of Austin's room followed by their dogs. "Hey, Mom. Can we make some popcorn?" Adam asked.

"Sounds like you gotta go?" Blake asked.

"Yes, I gotta wrangle the twins into showers. See you Wednesday."

"I'm looking forward to it. Good night, beautiful."

"Good night." Marcy put her cell phone on the charger as a warm feeling spread through her. The moments of terror on the highway had already dissipated. Calling Blake had been a good idea.

CHAPTER 16

Marcy threw her balled up napkin at Blake. "That is not true!" she laughed. They were enjoying a quick bite at Rosa's Tex-Mex, a local favorite that served the best tacos in town and was just two blocks from the high school.

"I swear to God!" He had been telling her about the time he caught a burglar who had done a smash and grab on a jewelry store in Brooklyn. He just smashed the counter with a crow bar, grabbed a bunch of stuff and threw it into his bag. He ran to the door just as we arrived, and he must have thought it was open. The glass was so clean, he knocked himself out. Easiest collar I ever made. Read him his rights while he was unconscious on the floor."

"You must see a lot of crazy stuff in your line of work."

"Yes. Some crazier than others, and more so after I moved to Homicide."

Marcy shuddered involuntarily. She loved crime

books and crime dramas, but it had to be different seeing some of the insane things people did to one another with one's own eyes. "I am sure."

Marcy glanced at her watch. She needed to get the boys from conditioning. "So, Saturday, then?"

"Absolutely." He grinned, taking her tray from her and throwing the leftovers and wrappers in the trash. He was glad he had convinced her to come out for a quick bite. Dating a mom with kids wasn't easy. But he liked her. A lot. And if he had to work around her schedule and the boys' sports schedules, he gladly would. He had met them already, just a quick hello, and small talk about baseball. They seemed like great kids.

"The boys will love it," she assured him as he walked her to her car.

They made plans for a Saturday afternoon with the boys to play miniature golf at a place in Banderas. She had the boys for the weekend and didn't want to leave them with a babysitter again, so he suggested the group outing. She only hesitated a moment. He had met the boys already, and if she planned to continue to see him, and she wanted to, he would need to get along with her kids. She was nervous about it but felt it was the right decision. The boys knew she planned to continue to see him and had even asked her some questions about her first date. If they were younger, she may have kept it from them a while longer, but they were growing up fast.

* * *

"Loser buys the milkshakes," Adam announced. The boys had thoroughly enjoyed playing miniature golf with Blake and competing against him. He had given them a run for their money. Adam had won, scoring a two under par, Blake and Austin tied with one under, and Marcy had made them all laugh. She had started out great, but after twenty Wonders of the World, had scored a measly eight over.

"Fine!" Marcy declared, throwing up her hands while they stood in line at Dee's Ice Cream parlor next door.

"Two mint chocolate chips, one cookie dough, and one strawberry," Marcy ordered and stood to the side so the next customer could order.

While waiting in line to get their order, Blake suggested, "Hey, guys, how about that match on Rainbow Six tonight? I have no plans. I could hit up Angel and see if he can get on. You can play this weekend, can't you?" He looked at Marcy who nodded, smiling that he had remembered, and touched that he was taking an interest in her kids

"Sure!"

"That'll be a blast."

"Perfect, I can grade my papers while you guys play tonight. This way tomorrow I can break out Angel's old grill he left at the ranch. You guys have been after me to make my famous bacon burgers."

"Oh, yeah!" Austin pumped his hand in the air. "And you should invite Blake over. She makes a mean burger."

"Um, yeah, sure," Marcy stumbled, shocked at her son's invitation. "I mean if you have no plans."

"I can make it. What time?" Blake smiled as he handed her and Adam a mint chocolate chip milkshake and gave the cookie dough to Austin.

"Um, say two o'clock. We usually eat around four on Sundays. We have breakfast late, so we skip lunch."

"I can bring my potato salad. I can whip some up tonight before the match."

"Cool!"

With plans with Blake and the boys on Sunday, Marcy felt like she could pinch herself. The man was sexy as sin, made her dream of what ifs, and he fit into her little family like he was meant to be there. He gave her hope. Her heart beat faster each time he smiled at her. Her stomach knotted up before each kiss, and when he looked at her the way he was doing right now, butterflies swarmed in her belly.

Yes, he most certainly gave her the feels. There was no denying it. The last few weeks since meeting Blake had been amazing. Yup, Sunday could not come soon enough, she thought.

* * *

The barbecue went well. The boys played catch with Blake in the yard, and he showed them a new way to field grounders and helped Adam with his pitching. He even set up a makeshift target on one of the fences so Adam could practice getting different pitches inside the batter's box. The dogs fetched the tossed balls and brought them back for Adam to try again.

After eating and then feeding the dogs, the boys retired to play on their Xbox while she and Blake sat outside and enjoyed a cool glass of lemonade. They chatted and sipped their lemonades as the sun began its descent. He talked a bit about the case he was working on – an artist who had been murdered and left for dead not too far away. She remembered reading about it in the paper four years ago when the artist's body had been discovered by hikers. So many sad stories. The poor wife must have been so devastated by the news. Having your husband missing for over a year and not knowing what had happened. She shuddered at the thought of losing someone that way. Plus, the local news had recently been reporting a lot of new missing persons in the area as well. She prayed for the families of those that were missing, and prayed that the missing would be found safely.

When he changed the subject and asked her about school, she chatted about her lesson plans for the following week, and how she was trying to line up some writers to speak to one of her classes.

He glanced at his watch, and she wondered how long he would stay. They both had to work the next day but it was not too late yet.

"How about a stroll, Marcy?" he asked.

She remembered their last stroll. Her stomach knotted and she felt suddenly nervous, but she didn't know why. She was glad the dusk of night hid her rosy cheeks as she accepted the invitation.

She had been dreaming about being alone with him all week. The weekend had been wonderful, but they hadn't gotten a private moment since last Friday evening.

Marcy chose the path and took them down to the small man-made lake on the western side of the property. They would be out of eyesight of the boys in case Blake wanted to kiss her again.

And he did. The moment they were out of view of the house and behind a large old oak, he tugged on her hand which he had been holding and turned her toward him. The kiss wasn't tender, though, and she became breathless. Her hands reached up to cup his face and give back as much as he was giving. His tongue did such delicious things to her senses. She felt his hands slide down from her waist and settle on her hips. She groaned when he pulled her to him, a soft moan that expressed the need building inside her. When she felt his erection, a power surged inside her and instinct made her press into him harder.

He groaned. God, how he wanted this woman. He barely knew her after a few short weeks, but he had spent a lot of time thinking about her. The way she smelled, her curves, her breasts. His hands had a mind of their own, and he reached around to cup her ass, holding and squeezing each cheek. She pushed harder against him, and when the kiss broke, he reeled from desire.

"God, woman, you're beautiful. I can't wait until…" He ended his thoughts and saw her eyes widen. "No pressure. You let me know when you're ready."

Marcy appreciated his patience. But she wanted more with him. "Would you think less of me if I said I was?" She was wet from his kiss. It had been over three years since Troy had touched her.

Blake laughed, but it sounded rough. He fought for control. "If your kids weren't a football field away, woman…" He made it sound sexy. He *was* sexy. She felt the muscles under his t-shirt ripple. She slid her hands over his chest and felt him tense underneath.

Blake couldn't resist her, nor the need he saw in her eyes. He knew it matched his own. Her touch set his body on fire, and he stooped down for another kiss, then one hand slid under her blouse to cup a breast encased in a lacy bra. The mere thought of her in lace made him harder. He tweaked the nipple through the thin cloth, and she softly cried out in pleasure. He wanted to make her come for him. He knew he shouldn't. It was too soon. When he felt her hand fumble with the button and zipper on his jeans, he let his need take over.

He walked her backwards, so they were further into the wooded area. He pushed her back against the rough oak and deepened the kiss. With one arm around her back to stabilize her, he slid the hand holding her breast down to the simple skirt she wore. He grabbed the hem, tossed it up, and slid his hand up her thigh. The moon was out and gave him just enough light to see what he was doing. Pushing her panties aside, he slid two fingers into her already dripping seam and began to massage her clit until it puckered into a little ball of nerves. Marcy danced and squirmed under the ministrations, coming hard and fast. He swallowed her cries as she continued to jerk his shaft. He wanted to let loose and come, but he stopped her.

"I want to come inside you the first time, Marcy. You need to stop." He fought for control. There would be a first time, a second time, and many more, he promised himself.

"Are you sure?" she asked breathlessly, her chest heaving with her fast release.

The sight of her breathing hard made him ache to suckle those beautiful breasts. "Yes, er, no." He laughed but began to straighten her clothes, then his own.

Marcy laughed with him, feeling like a teenaged girl. She couldn't believe how bold she had been. But she had wanted him. And she wasn't a teenager any longer. There was no denying the powerful chemistry between them.

"The boys will be with Troy next weekend. He picks them up from baseball conditioning."

"I get off work at five. I will see you Friday."

CHAPTER 17

On the following Friday, Blake rushed home to change. His plan was to grab some things and head straight to Marcy's. Things had been progressing so well with her. Each time he was with her, he found himself more and more charmed by her. So, when he found her standing in front of his apartment door ready to knock, he was happily astounded.

"I thought I was meeting you at your place. To what do I owe the pleasure?" he asked, leaning down to give her a kiss on the cheek.

When Marcy saw his apartment door swing open, her heart beat wildly, and she regretted her impulsive action to seek him out. All week she had been thinking of this. Doing this. Being alone with him. She shook her head, "I shouldn't have come." She took a step back.

"Whoa, wait. Come in. I was going to change and meet you." He ushered her into the apartment and led her to the small kitchen table. He went over to the refrigerator and popped it open. "Afraid I only have water, beer, and orange juice. Not much else."

"Water's fine." Marcy took in her surroundings. She was surprised to see he had tastefully decorated it. One large massive sofa and TV took up the living room, but a few potted plants and wall art pulled the small apartment together. Pictures of his cousin and nieces and his parents sat in frames on a shelf and another shelf held his collection of books. The coffee table had files, a remote control, and a set of coasters. She looked beyond into his bedroom. The walls were painted a baby blue, and the bed had a dark blue comforter. She swallowed hard. Her mouth went dry. She picked up the bottle of water he had placed before her and took a sip.

"So, Marcy, what brings you by?" Blake asked loudly. He had asked her the question twice now, but she hadn't heard him.

"I wanted to be alone with you. I couldn't wait." She practically whispered the words. But, she wanted to be honest.

His gut clenched at her words, and he smiled. He could see she was second-guessing herself, but he was flattered. He had been dreaming about her all week, especially since Sunday. He wanted her. Bad. He was glad she felt the same way. But he wasn't going to rush her.

"I told you, Marcy, no rush. When you are ready."

She took another sip from her water bottle and licked her lips when a drop escaped. Then she turned

118

to him, and he saw her green eyes glow. They were full of need. Her next words shocked him.

"I am ready. I want you," Marcy declared, and this time he heard the note of strength and passion.

He took two steps toward her. She met him half-way. "If you want me to stop, Marcy, just say the word."

She shook her head in the negative. "I'm ready."

He didn't need to be told three times. With one fell swoop he picked her up and carried her to his bedroom. Once inside, he let her body slide down his, then took her sweet lips in a blazing kiss.

He felt her hands begin to work the buttons of his shirt, and he helped her. Her simple dark blue dress slid to the floor, and she pulled a stick out of her hair and let the brown curls tumble down over her shoulder.

Just liked he'd imagined, she looked good in nothing but lace. Watching her step out of her dress in his bedroom had him rock hard before he had his shirt and tie off. But he made quick work of undressing, while she kicked off her shoes. In his boxers, he reached for her once more and swung her into his arms and carried her to his bed, carefully placing her into the center.

Without hesitation, he removed his boxers and climbed in beside her. "I'm on the pill," she told him. She shook with nerves.

His answer was a growl. "So, you okay with no condom? I bought some just in case."

"Yes, I'm good."

He would take it slow. He knew it had been a while

for her. He also knew she was self-conscious, but he thought she was beautiful. He would show her how much now.

"You are so beautiful, Marcy. Just as I imagined. Better." He said the words huskily, and she could feel his hot breath on her neck. He licked at her, and nipped at her with his teeth, and he smiled that delicious, decadent smile as he pulled the cup of her bra down on one of her breasts. When his teeth gently rolled her nipple, she sharply took in a breath. It was like a powerful electric current coursed from her nipple to her core and caused every fiber of her being to hum in anticipation.

Blake broke the suction on her nipple with a resounding pop, then gave equal attention to her other breast as his hands splayed across her stomach and inched its way down to her panties. His hand slid underneath and found her wet and ready. He teased her for a bit, and when she began to writhe, he helped her remove her panties and positioned himself above her, after separating and kneeling between her thighs. "Are you ready?" he asked.

"Yes," she moaned. She had been waiting for this moment all week. To feel Blake's possession of her body. To feel the satisfaction of his fullness moving deep inside her. She arched up to greet him as he held his cock in one hand. She saw the small bead of pre-cum at the tip and had the urge to lick it off. She would indulge herself another time.

Blake placed the tip just inside her velvety pussy. He knew he would taste that nectar soon, but for now, he needed to be inside her. Make her his. Looking into her green eyes, he pushed inside her and watched the beautiful irises grow as he thrust deeper and felt her womanhood clasp around him. Once he was balls deep, he began to withdraw slowly, then push back into her. He slowly increased the tempo until she was clawing at his back with her pink fingernails and crying out her own release. Her pussy was weeping and his dick was hot and slick. He exploded in one final plunge and collapsed beside her, taking her with him so he was still inside her with her on top.

"It's not too much?" she asked of her weight.

"No, not at all. Never," he promised. He had heard her make remarks about her weight as women often did and made a mental note to work on building her self-esteem issue. She was beautiful to him. Every inch of her. A real woman.

When their heartbeats settled, he rolled her to her side. "Woman, that was the best damn homecoming I've had in years."

Marcy smiled and blushed at the same time. "I'm glad you appreciated it. I felt silly about it but planned to do it all week."

"Not silly at all. You can surprise me like that any time. Man, I don't want to get out of this bed all weekend."

Marcy's smile dropped a little as she made lazy circles with one fingernail across his chest. "I do have to head back home. I have to take the dogs out of the barn and feed them."

"Of course. How about I follow you out there? I

cleared my plans for the whole weekend." He clasped her hand, brought it to his lips, and kissed it.

Marcy was touched by the simple act of his kissing her hand. "Now that's an offer I can't refuse." The fact that he had cleared his entire weekend to spend with her warmed her heart even more.

* * *

As Marcy prepared to leave Blake's apartment, he promised to be right behind her. He showered quickly and packed a duffel bag. When he arrived at the ranch, he also carried a bag of groceries.

"I like to cook, so I picked up a few things. The duffel bag has some clothes. Hope that's okay?"

Marcy opened the screen door wider. "I have no plans this weekend other than taking care of Champ and Chewie."

He stepped inside her kitchen and dropped the grocery bag on the counter. He lifted the other hand with his duffel bag. His eyebrow arched up in question.

"Oh, yes. Right this way." She led the way to her bedroom, and he put the bag beside her dresser.

"Nice room," he commented, looking at the bed with clear intentions using it this weekend. "So, um, we will be sleeping here tonight, I guess?" Blake teased her.

Marcy laughed nervously. "Well, if you want to sleep, we can do that, too."

He laughed. He liked the way she surprised him.

"But yes, you are welcome to share this big bed with

me. The dogs sleep in the boys' rooms. Come, I'll give you a quick tour."

Marcy showed him the rest of her house. Now that the boys started high school, they had chosen to have separate bedrooms. Next to each of the boys' beds, Chewie and Champ were curled in the fetal position on a doggie bed on the floor, waiting for their young master's return. In the fourth bedroom, which was the smallest one, Marcy had set up her desk and had plans to use it as an office for herself. Blake imagined her toiling away, working on that novel she wanted to write.

"So, is this where you will be writing that novel of yours?"

"Yes, that's the plan. I've outlined it this week. I can't wait to start." Her words trailed after her as she led the way into the main two rooms of the house, a big country kitchen that overlooked a massive family room.

He sat on one of the stools at the kitchen counter. "It's sounds like a great concept. I can't wait to read it." He turned to her and said, "How about you show me where to put these items?" He tapped the grocery bag. "I'll make us some dinner. I brought steaks. Can I use the grill?"

"Absolutely. I cannot refuse a man who knows his way around a kitchen and wants to cook for me. I'll feed Champ and Chewie, then toss a salad for us." At the sound of their names, the dogs came trotting into the kitchen, ears perked up and waggin' their tails in anticipation of their dinner.

"Perfect. I did bring the fixings for a salad."

They worked together in her kitchen seamlessly like they had done it before a thousand times. Marcy brought the dogs outside while he started up the grill and joined her in the field. They tossed the frisbee to the dogs while both Champ and Chewie raced each other to get the prize first.

"The grill should be hot enough. Steaks will be ready in just a few minutes," he announced and headed back to the house while she let the dogs have some free time to take care of their business.

"I'll be right there to set the table," she called.

"Already done," he called back to her.

"Blake Levine, I must say, I could get used to having you around."

Troy had never been home to help prepare dinner let alone set the table. He barely made it on time to eat with them.

"Good, I'm glad. I like being around."

He winked, making her butterflies swarm. It reminded her of the delicious things they had done together just hours before. The things they would do later that night and possibly into tomorrow and even Sunday. She wondered how many clothes he had brought in that duffel bag of his for their impromptu weekend as she watched him put the steaks onto the grill.

"I'm just going to wash up," she told Blake as she passed him on the porch after she dealt with the dogs.

"Okay, babe. I'll be finished grilling in a minute."

Marcy smiled as the door flapped closed behind

her. This kind of domestic bliss was nothing like her previous relationship. All thoughts of Troy, burglaries, and car accidents seemed like a bad dream when Blake was around.

* * *

During the weekend they spent a great deal of time in her big comfy bed, making love in ways Marcy hardly imagined. In between bouts of lovemaking, they spent time outdoors playing with the dogs, sitting in the rockers and talking, and walking the property.

"I've always wanted to have such a great piece of land. Ride ATVs, fishing. You have it all right here." He spread his arms out, indicating everything the ranch had to offer.

"Yes, Angel made a nice spot out here. But Jemma's place is twice as large and has a lot of land. Angel has been helping her renovate it. As a vet, it is perfect for him. So, I'm glad he decided to rent the ranch to me with the option to buy. ATVs would be cool for the twins. They would never want to come indoors. They would have the lay of the land in no time."

"Hey, if you're okay with it, maybe I could rent some for the weekend. I saw a sign out by the Honda dealership that they do that kind of thing."

"Oh, they would love that." Marcy made a mental note to talk to Troy about Christmas. She clearly couldn't afford ATVs, but he might want to be extra generous with them this year.

"Have they gone fishing yet in the lake?"

"Yes, but so far not a bite. Angel was working on stocking it, then Jemma came along. He says there are fish, but it'll take a few more years before we will be able to make a good day of it."

Blake nodded. Fishing on a lake outside your front door sounded like a dream.

"How about we head back and see about lunch?" he suggested when the sun began to climb down the other side of day. Regret that one of the greatest weekends of his life was coming to an end filled his eyes. However, he thought it best to leave before Marcy's ex-husband showed up at dinnertime with the boys.

"That sounds good." Marcy got up off the log where she perched and took his proffered hand.

The moment he stepped onto the porch his phone rang. One quick glance at the screen told him he needed to take it. "Sorry, Marcy, gotta take this. It's a work thing."

"No problem, I'll get started on lunch. Take your time."

Blake slid the ACCEPT CALL button over. "Hey, Snake. What can I do for you?"

"It's not what you can do for me, but what I can do for you." The biker's voice sounded like sandpaper, rough and scratchy.

Shit. Well, that didn't sound good. "What's up, Snake?"

"The girl. The blonde. She showed up in a bar some of my bikers were at last night. Comes on to one of my crew, a guy who goes by Wrenches." Blake briefly imagined why. "She was flashing all she was worth to

126

Wrenches and then same deal happens. Asks him if she can off someone for her."

"Where? You get a name?"

"At Boots in Banderas."

"I know the place. You got a name?" he repeated the question.

"Come by our place. I got Wrenches with me now, and he can fill you in with the particulars. You're going want to hear this in person."

"I'll be right over. Got an address for me?" Snake told him the location of the Dirty Bastards' Biker Club. "See you in thirty minutes."

"Not before we see you," the club's president said and hung up.

Blake needed the information these bikers seemed willing to give, but he had dealt with MCs before in New York. It could get tricky. It was always on their terms. He headed inside to grab his gear and let Marcy know he needed a raincheck on lunch.

CHAPTER 18

Blake arrived at the location provided by Snake's directions. Outside the wooden structure, a sign over the door bore the name of the MC club. Two bikers sitting outside, unpatched, kept watch. "Blake Levine," he introduced himself. "Snake called me."

One of the bikers looked him up and down, then rose from his chair and said, "Follow me."

The old building was well taken care of inside. Never judge a book by its cover, he reminded himself. A short hallway led to a set of swinging doors that opened into what looked to be a pool hall with two pool tables center stage and a bar alongside one wall. There were also several casual seating areas throughout the room. One lone woman, pretty, mid-thirties, tatted up, sat behind the bar and smoked cigarettes. She didn't even look up from the magazine she was reading.

"We're a small outfit, but a lot of the guys don't

come in on Sundays, and if they do, it's usually pretty late."

Blake absorbed the information as it could come in handy someday and continued to follow the younger biker.

"Snake's over there." The man before him pointed to a set of wooden doors across the room. "He's in the office with his VP and Wrenches." The biker didn't expect an answer from Blake. When he reached the doors, he tapped loudly.

"Come in," announced Snake from the other side. Blake turned the door knob and entered.

"Levine, come in." Snake greeted him like they were old friends. He sat at the head of a large rectangular table.

Blake was in the inner sanctum. Bikers often didn't invite cops to their clubhouses, so Blake treated the man and the room with the respect due the invitation.

"Thanks for inviting me, Snake."

"Sit, sit," he commanded and Blake sat down next to one of the other two bikers in the room. "This here next to me is Mad Dog, he's my VP, and you got Wrenches on your left." The man next to him, Wrenches, sported a full six-inch black beard, but his head was shaved completely bald.

"Nice to meet you both." Blake shook his head in the direction of each of the men.

"We have a small organization here. We're just bikers, Levine, who love to hang out. We get rowdy sometimes, but we keep our noses clean," Snake told him.

"I understand," Blake replied, knowing the man was testing him before he allowed Wrenches to speak with him. Blake would take the man at his word, unless he heard otherwise.

"Now we got that settled, we wanted to share this information with you. We respect the law in these parts. Go ahead," he gave Wrenches permission, "and tell the man what you told me. He's got no time to waste sounds like."

Blake looked to his left to hear Wrenches' story. "Well, like Snake told you, this girl was hitting on me pretty hard last night. Blonde, sexy as hell. I noticed her right away before she even laid eyes on me. She and her man were fighting, and he walks out. That's when she went on the prowl. I was totally okay with that. Her pussy is as good as the next, and she was a fine-looking piece of ass. She told me her name was Danielle, but that's all I got out'a her. At the time, I really didn't care what her last name was if you know what I mean."

Blake smiled and encouraged him to continue. Danielle. It was a start.

"Well, I bought her a few drinks, and she was all over me. We're sitting in the back, and I wanted to take her outside to finish what she started. But Danielle grabs my cock, whispers in my ear, and asks me if I'm man enough to take someone out for her." Wrenches looked angry recounting that part. "No fucking woman asks me if I'm man enough when she's got my hard cock in her hands. That shit don't fly."

"What happened after that?" Blake asked.

"Well, I don't do that kind of shit, first off. I ain't no hired killer. I had heard about what happened to Snake a month ago. So, I know this has to be the same woman, put two and two together. I knew the sheriff would be interested in knowing more, so I played along with it. I told her, 'You got my hard cock in your hand. I think you can tell what kind of man I am'."

"Okay." Blake liked where it was going but hoped Wrenches had more information than just a first name, if the woman had even used her real name. "What else were you able to find out?"

"'Fraid not much more. I told her to keep talking and rubbing my dick. I might consider it. I asked, 'Do you need me to off your old man? Is he hitting you?' And she fucking starts laughing at that."

"That's strange."

"Yeah, I thought so, too. Almost made my dick go soft. Almost." Mad Dog laughed and Wrenches winked at him but kept talking. "But no, she tells me she needs a WOMAN to be hit. I was like what the fuck a woman do to you that you want her dead?" His expression was one of shock. "We got a code here, and we don't hurt women. No fucking way, but I was actually curious at this point so I kept at it."

Blake was glad he did, too. "Go on."

"Well, the fucking bitch was cold. Stone cold. She was like, 'It's all about the money, honey, and I gotta get rid of the bitch to get what's mine'."

Blake wasn't as shocked as Wrenches that Danielle's target was a woman. He'd heard stories of siblings offing each other over inheritances or business partners who wanted the entire company for themselves.

"Fucked, up shit, right? So I asked who the mark was. I wanted the particulars."

Blake liked this. He knew if he had the name of the mark, he would be able to find the would-be assassin.

"She tells me it's her man's soon-to-be ex-wife, some teacher, and then this other guy comes storming in and yanks her out of the seat. It was the guy who left her there. Said he changed his mind and he would do it. She left with him saying, 'I knew you would come back to your senses.'"

Blake's stomach lurched and he wanted to bolt out of his seat, but he kept his cool and listened, waiting for Wrenches to finish his story. The description of the mark was hitting close to home. Marcy was in the middle of a divorce. Could it be? "What did this other man look like?"

"He was tall, blond hair, a bit older. I'm bad with ages. She was in her mid to late twenties, but he was definitely older than that."

"Thank you," Blake said, standing.

Snake looked confused. "You got everything you need here?"

"Yes, unless you followed them and saw their vehicle?" Wrenches shook his head and looked down at his crotch. Blake was disappointed. He wondered if a dark blue pickup might be what they drove off in. He knew he was jumping to conclusions and needed hard facts. "Okay, well if you think of anything else, you have my number. Snake, can I call if I need to talk to Wrenches here?"

"Yes, and thanks for asking. You call me and I call him. Sometimes he's running errands for me." Snake winked, making Blake wonder what kinds of errands.

"Gotcha." Blake nodded, beginning to understand the relationship and the work that was done at Dirty Bastards. They lived pretty close to the border. "I do appreciate this information. You've helped a great deal."

Blake was escorted out of the building by the same unpatched biker who had brought him in. His mind spun in different directions and cold fear swept through him. Bits and pieces of information started to click. A teacher. Marcy. It could be a huge coincidence or Marcy was in danger.

Once inside his car, Blake hesitated before starting up the vehicle. "Who the hell is Danielle? And this other man?" he asked aloud.

Could it be fathomable this teacher who had a soon-to-be ex was Marcy? His Marcy. She was in the middle of a divorce and had described her ex's new girlfriend as a blonde Barbie doll. His instincts kicked into high gear. Cops didn't believe in coincidences and there were just too fucking many pointing in a direction he didn't like.

Was Marcy the potential victim here? Was he thinking clearly because in the past month he had been falling for her? He had a lot of work to do. And for starters he would need to investigate Nancy and the good doctor. Just in case. He turned the ignition on and the vehicle roared to life. Images of Marcy popped into his head. The burglary, the incident while driving home. Were they actual coincidences? Or something more sinister? His foot hit the gas, and he knew he wouldn't be headed home. Not tonight. He needed to use the sheriff's office computers to get the information he wanted. He might be jumping to the wrong conclusion, but nothing mattered except keeping Marcy safe. Her and her kids.

Blake had to figure out Danielle's identity. He had a first name. Now, he needed a last name. Was Danielle an alias for Nancy? He knew he couldn't lay blame at her feet, not without proof, or make assumptions about the good doctor, Adam and Austin's father. He didn't even know if the good doctor fit the description of the other man. He needed to do some digging before he made any accusations. Not until he had solid evidence.

Fuck. Was he barking up the wrong tree? He didn't know. Was he too close? he asked himself. Fuck. Marcy. Well, whether she liked it or not, she would be seeing a lot more of him until he was certain whether or not she was the target of this murder-for-hire plot. Accusing her ex of something so horrible without proof would destroy what they had begun. He didn't want that. For now, though he hated to do it, he needed to keep his suspicions from Marcy.

His relationship with her had just become a whole heck of a lot more complicated.

CHAPTER 19

The fall in Texas was her favorite time of year. Marcy floated on cloud nine as Halloween approached. It was Friday, and though she could have left sooner as Troy had the weekend with the boys, she waited in the parking lot of her high school. When she saw his vehicle, she got out of hers.

She had been texting with Blake who was on his way to her house, he'd told her. He spent every weekend with her and the boys. Blake didn't sleep over when the boys were home, but he stayed late and then usually arrived first thing in the morning. They had gone fishing and ATVing together twice. Other times they stayed indoors, ate pizza, and played board games. One Saturday night Marcy beat them soundly in Monopoly by bankrupting them all, which she claimed gave her boasting rights.

Troy had texted her earlier that day wanting to talk with her. Another mediation meeting was coming up, and he wanted to discuss it with her beforehand. So, she had waited.

She was slightly miffed when she noticed that Barbie was with him. Thankfully, the woman remained in Troy's canary yellow jeep. More sensible than picking up the boys in the BMW.

She met Troy halfway and Nancy waved from her open window. Marcy waved back, though she couldn't force a sincere smile.

"Thanks for meeting with me." Troy ran his hands though his thinning blond hair. He did that when he was nervous. "Marcy, I need you to accept my final offer next week. I don't want this case dragging out in the courts and I suspect neither do you."

"I will if I have to, Troy. You know very well what you have offered so far is a pittance of what I am due, and I am not even asking for that much. I mean I'm not asking for any of the investments we made, the ROTH..."

Troy cut her off. "Nancy's pregnant."

Marcy's mouth dropped at the bombshell. Flabbergasted, congratulations didn't seem to be the right thing to say. Not by the look of Troy's face. She knew for a fact he didn't want more kids. He had told her several times to be careful with her birth control over the years when she had let her prescription lapse.

"Um..."

"Yeah, I know. Not expected. Not planned. But I hear from the boys you have a new boyfriend, so I know you want this done soon, too."

"Yes, but we aren't rushing into anything. He is

aware of my situation," Marcy defended her relationship.

"Well, Nancy wants to get married before she starts showing too much. What I can offer is all you've asked for, but I need the house proceeds. The condo will be too small. I can offer you an additional hundred thousand. You'll have half what you need for the ranch, and you can easily get a mortgage for the rest."

"That's not fair, Troy. I'll have to live paycheck to paycheck with that kind of mortgage. What about your investments?"

"I can't touch those. The penalties and the taxes I'll pay will hurt my portfolio. You know I'll help when you need it," he argued.

"I don't know," Marcy hedged. "Can I think about it?" She really didn't want to go that low. She had hoped to buy the small ranch outright. Her salary would cover the bills, and there would be a little extra each month for her to start saving and maybe do some fun things with the boys from time to time. She didn't want to have to ask for money from her ex if she wanted to do something special.

"Yes, please. Think about it. Thank you." His face relaxed somewhat and he turned and waved at Nancy.

Marcy hid her ire at the exchange. Her woman's intuition told her Nancy was pushing him hard to get the divorce done, but with him on the winning side. She may have her own money like Troy said, but it didn't stop Marcy from thinking the woman wanted more.

Nancy got out of the car at that moment and began

to approach them. Her hand went instinctively to her flat belly and Marcy inwardly winced. Her sons would share a sibling with this woman. Lord, help her!

"Hi, I'm Nancy." The woman put out her hand. "We really haven't met formally, and I totally get that, but since the divorce is moving in the right direction, soon we'll put this behind us and be one big happy family."

Marcy dropped the woman's hand quickly after she took it. The woman made sure her hand turned over so Marcy could see the ring Troy had purchased for her. "Yes, well, as I told Troy, I will think about his offer and let him know in mediation next week."

"Perfect. Oh, I wanted to tell you what great boys you have. So polite and well-mannered. Troy keeps telling me it was all you, how good they turned out."

"Thank you," Marcy accepted the offhanded compliment. "They have their moments."

"Yes, Marcy. You did do a great job with them," Troy added.

"Thank you. Yes, they seem to be much better now that the twin terror phase has passed." In middle school, Marcy thought some days the devil was in them due to the amount of mischief they had gotten into.

Troy smiled. "I told you they would outgrow that."

"True. You did." Marcy smiled, remembering those conversations with Troy. They may not have had the best personal relationship, but when it came to the kids, they had always been on the same page.

Nancy interrupted the moment. "Did they tell you we went horseback riding last weekend and want to take them camping next weekend on Halloween?"

That was Marcy's weekend. "I…"

"Yes, sorry, Marcy. I meant to mention it," Troy interjected. Then he turned to Nancy. "I hadn't gotten around to that part, Nance. It slipped my mind for a moment." Troy paused and met Marcy's direct gaze. "I was wondering if we could have this weekend and next. Then you can have them two weekends in a row."

Marcy wanted to escape. She started to feel something bubble up inside her. "I guess so."

Nancy clapped her hands gleefully. "We'll go hiking near William's Creek, and maybe even go horseback riding again. I used to go there a lot when I was a kid."

Marcy had enough chit-chat for the day. "Okay, well, I guess goodbye then. See you Sunday, Troy. Nancy."

"And please think about the offer," Nancy added.

Marcy turned around and didn't acknowledge Nancy's last remark at all. She began walking to her car.

"It's for the best," Nancy called out after Marcy reached for the handle.

Once safely inside her vehicle, Marcy began to laugh. She didn't know why. Deep laughter rumbled up from somewhere and she had to let it out. She didn't know if it was shock or the look on Troy's face when he told her Nancy was pregnant. She watched as they both walked over to the practice field to collect the boys from their baseball conditioning. Something about the whole conversation struck her as funny as hell.

On Monday, she would call her lawyer and give him a heads-up about Troy's offer. She still didn't think it was doable. But she would think about it. She had promised.

CHAPTER 20

On Wednesday, Blake met Marcy at Rosa's Tex-Mex for a quick bite. He would go to her place later but needed to work a few hours at the office. He was finally making some headway in the cold case he had been working on for months. He had picked up the trail of the brother of the artist's wife, Noreen. Charles Hall. A highway patrol officer had arrested the brother and was going to call Blake about it in an hour when he started his shift in Oregon.

The thing that was really eating away at him, though, was his new case, and Danielle. He had made no headway locating her or the blond man who had been with her. He had checked for video, but again, the establishment had not finished fixing things up since the storm. Troy's driver license photo showed he was forty and blond. So older, but Blake didn't think he could pass for someone in his twenties. Nancy, on the other hand, could easily fit the bill of the description Wrenches had given him of Danielle. But, a working camera down the street hadn't been able to capture the entrance to the bar where the duo had been seen exiting. His examination into Nancy Reeves led nowhere. She was a debutante from the South who had gone to university in Texas. Family money kept her comfortable. He checked out her North Carolina roots, and according to his sources, the family was only too happy to support the woman away from home. A scandal with a local married politician had besmirched the family honor. Guess sleeping with married men was her modus operandi.

"Okay, darling." Marcy accepted the kiss on the cheek after Blake walked her to her car. "See you soon." She left to go pick up the boys with a bag of burritos and some chips with salsa they would probably gulp down in the car before making it home. "The boys want to watch a movie with you tonight. We will wait for you."

"All right, beautiful. I just need a couple of hours." He watched her drive off toward the school.

He was at his desk for only ten minutes when the call came in. "Levine," he answered.

"This is Highway Patrol Officer George Epson. You called wanting to know about an arrest I made a year ago, Charles Hall."

"Yes, sir. What can you tell me?"

"The man was weaving in and out of traffic. I pulled him over. He was with a woman, and from the look on her face they had been arguing. I asked to see the license, registration, and insurance information. Mr. Hall gave me his license and insurance card, but nothing on the vehicle. The woman explained it was her car. She had just moved from Texas and her things were being brought by the mover."

"Okay, but why did you arrest Hall?" Blake wanted to know. He also wondered if the woman had been Noreen.

"I went to run the car's license plate, and from my vehicle I saw him backhand the woman, so I got out of my patrol car and arrested the man on the spot. Once at the station, the woman, of course, refused to press charges against her husband, so we couldn't hold him."

"So, the woman in the vehicle was his wife?" Noreen was supposed to be his siter. He blinked. Not related. This put a new spin on things.

"Claimed to be. I had them down at the station, and the woman was begging me the whole time to let him go, so I eventually did. Nothing we can do if they won't press charges, said she had asked for it which is bull-shit. Anyhow, I cited them for not having the vehicle registration, and gave them a ticket saying they needed to pay the citation and provide proof of ownership. They did neither so it got flagged in the system. I was pissed as hell when they didn't make the court date, and so I did some digging. The car, turns out, didn't belong to either of them. They lied to me. Fucking thing was reported stolen in Texas. I couldn't believe I let them go. So, I did some more digging. A college student named, wait, let me see. Yes, here it is. Nancy Reeves reported it stolen four years earlier."

Blake almost fell out of his chair. How and the hell did Noreen and Charles Hall have Nancy's car? He started to shake after he ended the call with Epson. His mind was going in a million directions. He had never expected his cold case and current case would somehow become mixed up together. What the hell was going on? How the hell did Nancy Reeves' car get stolen by the people he was looking to question in his cold case on Cole Lansing? Did she know them? He needed to dig deeper into Nancy and Charles and Noreen. He hadn't gone deep enough. Something clicked. He looked up his contact in the Carolinas and called him. "I need to see some pictures of Nancy Reeves. Can you send me her North Carolina driver's license?"

"Give me ten minutes. I'm walking into my office now."

"Thanks."

He hung up with him and pulled up the Cole Lansing file. He flipped through some pages and could not find a photo of Noreen. He had a grainy image from the funeral and one from a missing person's flyer, but she was wearing a veil at the funeral. On the photo of her from the flyer she was with her husband Cole, but she wore big sunglasses that hid half her face. He flipped a few more pages. There was note about Noreen not having a driver's license as she had never bothered to get one growing up in the city. The friend. Lisa. He pulled out her contact information.

"Lisa, Deputy Levine. Yes, the same." She remembered him. He got to the point. "Do you have any pictures on your phone of Noreen and her brother Charles?"

"Um, I think so. I'd have to scroll through a lot of photos on my phone. Oh shoot. Wait, I got a new phone last year, and there was a problem with transferring the data because I had dropped mine in the swimming pool."

"What about social media? Did you post any pictures of the two of you?"

"You know, Deputy, I did, and Noreen got mad. I had to take them down. She said her folks were vicious, so she left home when she was eighteen. She didn't want them being able to track her down. I forgot all about that."

"Did you develop any pictures?" He was desperate for a photo of Noreen Hall-Lansing.

"I'm afraid not."

He hung up with her after securing a promise to see if any of their mutual friends might have one. He looked at the image of the brother, Charles, he had gotten from the arrest report in Oregon. He was twenty-seven at the time of the arrest. What had he done to his sister or wife? Who was the woman in the car? Had it been Noreen?

Just as he sat back to think, he noticed he had received an email from his friend in North Carolina. Nancy Reeves' driver's license appeared on the screen moments after he double clicked to open the image. He almost fell out of his seat when the woman in the picture looked hardly anything like the Nancy Reeves who was living with Marcy's ex. True, the girl in the photo had been a teenager then. Both blonde, but nothing should change that much in nearly a decade.

Nancy must have had a lot of work done. Her lips were much fuller, eyebrows higher. Nose thinner. But the eyes looked somewhat the same. It was the shape and color. The Texas driver's license showed an older woman and did not match the one from North Carolina at all. However, all the other details matched. Same university, same social security number.

Hell's bells. Was the Nancy Reeves the same person on the two driver's license photos? He couldn't be sure. And if the woman engaged to Dr. Field's wasn't the same woman, where and the hell was the real Nancy Reeves? And who the hell was the woman living with Dr. Fields? He had too many unanswered questions and knew he needed to talk to Jack, but he had taken the evening off. He would get him on the phone first thing in the morning.

He also knew he needed to talk to Marcy. He couldn't keep his suspicions to himself any longer. The woman spending so much time with her boys was not the person she appeared to be, and he had to let Marcy know. She would never forgive him if he held something back that could possibly put her boys in jeopardy.

Not knowing what he was going to say, Blake grabbed his keys after locking up his files. He needed to think of something quick that would make sense to Marcy. But nothing was making sense to him right now. He wondered once more for the millionth time in the last hour if he was too close to this thing. Like hell was he taking a step back though. He was not letting anything happen to Marcy on his watch. She and her kids meant far too much to him.

He knew he was in deep.

When Blake pulled up in front of Marcy's house, he was no closer to figuring out what he was going to tell her. Halfway there, he called Jemma and asked if she was busy. He thought she might need a friend later, and he also needed someone to occupy the boys while he talked to Marcy.

Jemma pulled up behind him with Angel in tow as Marcy emerged from the house. She must have seen their cars approach or the new security system alerted her on her phone.

"Everything all right?" Marcy asked, noticing the concerned looks on their faces. She wiped her wet hands on the dishtowel she was holding.

Jemma shrugged and looked at Blake for an answer. "I don't know. Blake said he needed to talk to you alone, and asked me if I could watch the boys for a bit."

A cold sweat broke out on Marcy's brow. She turned to Blake. "Blake, everything okay with us?"

He heard the worry in her voice and hated she had doubts about them.

"You're still my girl," Blake said and put his heart into the words so she knew he meant them. "It's about the burglary and car accident and some cases I am working on. I think they may be related."

Her expression changed from worry to confusion. "Okay, well, let me tell the boys that Angel and Jemma are here, and then I'll be right out." Marcy ducked back into the house to speak with the boys.

"Actually, if you don't mind, Angel, maybe Jemma can hang back with us? Marcy might need a friend after she hears all this."

"Well, I don't know about that." Angel stepped forward. "This ain't putting Jemma in danger is it?" he asked.

Blake respected the man even more for asking that question. "No, man, I swear. It's about moral support-- moral support woman to woman."

"Okay, man. I will trust you on this."

"Jemma will fill you in. Promise."

Angel nodded and went inside. "Homework, how boring," Blake heard Angel announce exuberantly. "How about Rainbow Six, boys, when you finish? That okay, Marcy?"

"Yes, just this once," he heard Marcy say on her way out the door. She was pulling on a sweater to block out the chill and the worry she felt.

"Let's go down by the lake so the boys don't over- hear," Blake suggested. With both women following him, he continued, "I don't want to worry them or you both, for that matter, but some unusual things have come up in an investigation, actually two investiga- tions, I'm working on. I want to tell you as much as I can, but please know, Marcy, I can't tell you all of it because they are active investigations."

The women followed him to the lake. "I thought you said this was about the burglary and the car acci- dent," Marcy murmured.

"What's going on?" Jemma demanded. "You're scaring Marcy." She saw Marcy shivering.

"Frankly, I'm scared, too. Fuck. I know I am handling this all wrong, but sit, please, ladies, and I will explain what I can."

Blake started by explaining that after Marcy's burglary and car accident he did some digging on her ex and his girlfriend because he was overly worried about her.

"You think they had something do with the burglary? That's ridiculous. Troy would never..."

"I know. I was working another case, a murder-for-hire thing, and being overly protective, an abundance of caution, I had to check. I was being a cop, Marcy, please don't be mad. It's who I am. I care about you so just want to make sure your safe. I didn't find anything suspicious about Nancy at first, so I let it go, just kept her on my radar because of my feelings for you."

"Okay," Jemma encouraged. "He cares about you. He's a deputy, that is how their minds work."

Blake was grateful for her defense of him. "I didn't say anything because I thought it was a stretch myself. It was just me being cautious."

Marcy gave him a measured look before she continued. "Okay, I appreciate it. But why the renewed fear?"

Blake jumped in with the latest developments. "I can't say much about my ongoing cases, but during the course of the investigations, Nancy Reeves' name came up and it floored me."

"Wait? What? A completely different crime?" Marcy was shocked. "So, she's a criminal?"

"I don't know that yet, but I do know two people I am looking for were driving a car she reported stolen last year. And," he hesitated before revealing the last bit, "I'm not a hundred percent sure her real name is Nancy Reeves."

"Wait. Hold up!" Jemma exclaimed, throwing both her hands in the air. "This makes no sense."

"The pieces haven't clicked yet. I'm close. I'm on to something big here. I know it. I dug into her past, learned some things about her life in North Carolina, an inappropriate relationship with a friend of the family at a tender age, her getting shipped off to school here and being told to stay in Texas and the checks will keep coming. But my buddy in North Carolina sent me her driver's license, and she does not look much like the Nancy Reeves living with your ex."

"What? Why? Could there be two Nancy Reeves?" Marcy asked.

"People change in ten years," Jemma added.

"True. But then she has had a lot of cosmetic surgery. And I don't know if I am dealing with two different Nancy's, but they are both using the same social security number. Something is off with this Nancy. I don't like the idea of the boys being alone with her for now, Marcy and that is why I wanted you to know."

Marcy was biting her nail. A bad nervous habit. She pulled her finger from her mouth. "Yes, I agree." Marcy started to pace instead.

He added the final words he had been holding back. "Especially if this Nancy is associated with either one of my cases, the murder-for-hire, or the woman whom I think killed her husband."

Marcy stopped cold. "You think she is...Oh my God! What am I going to do? They are supposed to go hiking this weekend with Troy and whoever the hell she is." Marcy flailed her arms.

Blake reached her in two strides. He put his hands on her arms to still her. "I'm volunteering over at the animal sanctuary; Jack's woman is doing a big event over at her place for the locals. How about telling the boys you really wanted to take them there, and it's your weekend? It may sound petty, but I don't think they should be with Nancy for the foreseeable future, and you can't tell Troy as it is an active investigation. I'm close, Marcy. I will figure this out soon. I promise."

"What about the weekend after that? And after that? Whatever is going on, Troy may have his faults, but I can't keep his boys from him forever."

Jemma suggested, "You could say something happened to your sister next weekend. Your folks. We will think of something. Take it one weekend at a time."

"That could work." Marcy continued to bite her nail.

Blake couldn't stand the fear he saw in her and needed to hold her. He pulled her to him.

"I'm right here beside you, beautiful. I am not going anywhere, and I promise not to let anything happen to you or your boys. I will have some deputies watching them when they are out of sight. Whatever it takes." Her arms reached around him and she pressed closer tunneling in.

"Thank you, Blake. For everything. For your honesty. It is so refreshing. I know it wasn't easy coming out here and telling me all of this. I know you weren't supposed to, either. But I am glad you did."

Blake felt her heart beating rapidly in her chest. He wondered if she felt his heart beating just as quickly, just as loudly. In fear, for her.

He kissed the top of her head, and knew in that moment how much he loved this brave, beautiful woman. He would do anything to keep her and her kids safe.

Anything at all.

CHAPTER 21

Blake's training with the TVFD was going well. Along with many of the other the new guys, he was busy getting his training in and volunteering to work at community events. He was excited about the big Halloween event that day. The woman in Jack's life, Justice McAlester was sponsoring the event on her land on the outskirts of Tarpley. His cold case was finally bringing in some new leads, and he felt like things between him and Marcy were going extremely well. He smiled thinking about last night. Yes, they were both on edge due to recent events, but even that had just served to bring them closer together.

Her kids were great. Close to their mother, he knew that came from great parenting and her spending quality time with them. He loved being included in some of their plans together. He had no siblings of his own, no nieces or nephews. He loved the whole family "vibe". True, she was still married, and that was a complication, but from the sounds of it, she was well on her way to finalizing her divorce thankfully. She was special, and he could see having her in his life full-time. He wasn't ready yet to use the 'L' word on her, but he was definitely feeling it.

When Blake got to Justice's place around noon, things were already in full swing. It looked like many volunteers and TVFD personnel had shown up earlier to prepare. He saw Justice off in the distance, talking to a small group of people. She pointed in different directions, obviously assigning jobs. There were lots of these events in Tarpley and the surrounding areas. That was another thing he was beginning to love about Texas. Each community was an extended family.

Blake saw several people he recognized already working as he made his way over to Justice.

"Here you go, Blake." A woman he did not know, but obviously knew him, handed him a cup of hot cider.

"Thanks," he replied, but the woman was already moving on, passing out more containers of warm cider to other volunteers.

He continued on his journey and saw Jemma and Angel. They were setting out trash cans in designated locations from a flatbed loaded with blue barrels, some marked as trash and others as recycling. From the number on the flatbed, Justice must be expecting a large turnout. He saw Tank, too. Tank had trained the guys on the main engine last weekend and was the same Tank who had towed Marcy's car and gave her a loaner after her hit-and-run.

Tank was lifting bales of hay out of a pickup like they were feather pillows. He was with Calliope who worked with Marcy and Jemma. She directed where the bales were placed--around a grassy area near the porch for people who needed a rest. He noticed the beverage table also being set up nearby.

Blake walked towards Justice after giving Angel a friendly nod and waving to Jemma when he caught their eyes. It was going to be a long day, and he would be there until the end. He was glad Marcy was planning on bringing the boys later that night. She said she'd come by around eight o'clock. Though the boys had been upset about not being able to go camping and hiking with their dad near William's Creek, she knew they would have fun tonight.

"Hi, Blake. Thanks for coming out," Justice greeted him as he approached her on the left. She swung her long, dark hair out of her face.

"Not at all. Looks like everything is running smoothly so far. Where do you need me?"

"I would like you and Rodriguez to work traffic control and the parking lot." She pointed across the field where Rodriguez was hammering a wooden post into the ground. From this distance, he saw Rodriguez had a wheelbarrow full of them.

"No problem." This was something he had done before at many New York city events. "I got it covered."

"Rodriguez has some twine and posts. He's already started laying out a grid. But here," she reached into her pocket and pulled out a couple of rolls of reflective parking tape. "I forgot to give him these. Put pieces on the posts and anywhere else you think they need to be."

"Gotcha," he replied. He knew the tape would come in handy when it got dark. It would help people navigate their way off the field they were parking in come nightfall and prevent cars from getting accidentally dinged when people rounded corners or backed up. "I'll get to work. This looks like a lot of fun," Blake said. "My…friend, Marcy Fields, is bringing her boys. I think the twin terrors will really enjoy the hayride. It's wonderful of you to put on this event."

"The more the merrier. Do her sons go to Bandera High School?"

"No. She teaches at Medina."

"Ah." Justice considered a moment. "Wait, is she married to Dr. Fields?"

Blake shifted from one foot to the other. He felt uncomfortable talking about Marcy's business with others, and though his boss Riggs was aware of the situation, he didn't know how much he'd told Justice, if anything, of their complicated relationship. He also knew a lot of people didn't look too kindly on a man who was dating a married woman, albeit, separated and soon-to-be divorced woman. "Sort of," he mumbled lamely, but then made his excuse to get away from what had turned into an awkward conversation. "Time to get to work. Call if you need me." He patted the radio at his side.

* * *

By the time Marcy was set to arrive, Blake looked around at what the volunteers had accomplished under Justice's direction. The ranch had been transformed into a Halloween night of fun and terror. There were tractors ready to pull hay-filled wagons. Volunteers donned scary and horror-themed costumes to make the night spooktacular. Pop-up ghosts, witches, and demons had been set up all over the property to be triggered when people walked past them. There was even an area designated as a petting zoo for the little ones, and the maze, of course, for those who dared to brave it. Warning signs about zombies and murderers on the loose, cobwebs hanging from trees and branches, and smog machines added to the overall effect. Even eerie sounds punctuated the air by hidden speakers scattered about the site of the event.

The most terrifying sound of all, in Blake's opinion, was the wolf recording. The first time Blake heard it, he actually froze in disbelief and reached for his weapon, which was safely locked in his vehicle. It had given him a fright, sounding so incredibly real.

Rodriguez jumped, too, and they looked at each other sheepishly.

"What, New York? Scared of a little old wolf?" he teased.

Blake laughed. "I won't tell if you don't."

Rodriguez cracked a toothy grin. "Deal."

They both laughed and shook off the terror of the woeful sound. They continued to work together, seamlessly directing the incoming and outgoing traffic.

They had donned reflective vests since dusk and were using small flashlights to help direct traffic.

Blake was beginning to worry though. It was only half past eight, but Marcy hadn't shown up yet with Adam and Austin. He checked his cell to see if she had texted him that she was going to be late. Nothing. So, he sent her a quick message asking if she was on her way.

"Everything okay?" Rodriguez asked sometime later.

"I don't know," he murmured distractedly, checking his phone again for messages. Nothing. It was past nine now. Maybe it was his cop's instinct, but something didn't feel right.

"Come on, New York." Rodriguez clapped him on the back. "Spill it."

He relented. "It's Marcy. She was supposed to be here an hour ago. She hasn't answered my calls or texts."

Rodriguez knew what was going on with his cases. "Go check on her. Tell Justice I can handle it. Traffic coming in has slowed enough I can handle the parking on my own."

"You sure?"

"Yes. Go," Rodriguez ordered.

Blake found Justice at the admissions table as people waited to have their hands stamped for the event. She was busy, but when she saw him approach, she gave him her attention.

"Problem?" she asked.

"Not sure. Marcy hasn't shown up and I can't get her on her cell."

"Yikes. That's not good."

"Yeah. Not like her."

Justice glanced around. "We're covered here. Go check on her. Maybe she had car trouble or something and her phone died."

He hoped like hell that was it. "You sure?" he asked one more time. He did not want to leave her shorthanded.

"I'm sure. Jack's out there playing Wolfman, Bandera PD is here, and Hank. Some of the other guys from TVFD said they'd stop by too... We're good. Go!"

"Going." He turned on his heel and trotted to his vehicle. Something was making his cop senses tingle.

"Hope everything's okay and she's just running late. Call me if you need anything!" Justice called after him.

"Will do." He jumped into his vehicle.

As he drove past Rodriguez, his cell phone rang. Relief swept through him when he recognized the caller ID. He hit the button on the steering wheel to take the call over the vehicle's Bluetooth.

"Marcy, everything okay?" he asked, getting straight to the point.

"No, it's not."

He could hear the note of fear in her voice. He stepped on the gas. "I'm headed your way now. What happened?"

"I'm not home. I went to pick up the boys from baseball conditioning at five and they were not there. The coach said they didn't attend conditioning and that they were picked up by their dad after school. They told some friends they were going camping. They lied to me and told their father I had changed my mind and said they could go."

"Okay, so where are you?" Blake asked, decelerating.

"I'm at the William's Creek campsite. It's in the other direction."

"I know where it is." Blake turned around. He had just passed the turn off to William's Creek. "I'm not far. Maybe fifteen minutes away."

Sobs came on the line. He heard her sniffle and get control of herself. "The boys are missing. Troy and Nancy are here. When I arrived, they said the boys went to the creek to get water, and when they did not come back within a few minutes, Troy went to look for them. He couldn't find them. They have been lost now for over two hours."

Blake didn't ask her why she hadn't called him sooner. She was clearly frantic. "I'm on my way, and I'm gonna call for backup," he promised. "I'll be there in ten minutes."

"Troy already called Conor, the local game warden. They are on the way."

"Good. I'll be there soon, baby. Hang on."

Blake knew the game warden and his team would know the area. He was closer but felt unsure of his ability to be of any great help. He knew very little of tracking, but Riggs did. He picked up his radio and made the call.

His boss answered right away. "Riggs."

"I…Sheriff..Blake. Levine."

"What's wrong?" Jack cut to the chase.

"I…Jack…can you come? I mean I know…Wolfman but…" He stammered, not able to think about anything other than getting to Marcy and finding someone who could help search for her boys.

"Where are you?" Jack demanded.

Blake let him know he was five minutes away from the William's Creek campsite. "It's Marcy. Her boys were camping there and went missing."

"I'll be there as quick as I can."

"I…thanks, Jack."

"S'what I'm here for." The radio went silent.

Blake was glad he had called him. Riggs knew this area better than anyone, according to most. He focused on making the turns, relieved to know Jack was only twenty minutes behind him.

When Blake parked next to Marcy's car, he spotted her right away. Her face was streaked with dirt and smudged makeup from her tears. Behind her was her ex-husband and Nancy. Nancy did not appear distraught. The doctor appeared just as worried as his wife.

Troy spoke as Marcy rushed into Blake's waiting arms. "I've gone back to the creek twice, but so far nothing. We have all gone out and looked, but didn't want to stray too far in case the boys came back or Conor and help arrived."

"Where have you looked?" Blake scanned the darkness.

"We've gone to the creek and walked it up and down, calling out for the boys, but so far nothing. They must have wandered too far to hear us."

"Did you see which direction they took? That they actually went to the creek?"

Marcy pointed toward the right. "The creek is that way. It's just a five-minute walk, but…" she let her voice trail off.

Troy shot Nancy a searing look. "I haven't been here before. My first time camping here. But Nancy said she had been. She pointed that way when we sent the boys off." He pointed not exactly west, but south-west. More south than west, Blake thought.

Nancy pouted like a child. "I told you, I'm sorry. I was confused. I guess I gave them the wrong location. They would have eventually hit the creek. It's been a long time since I have been here. Not since I was in college," she whined.

"But it veers about a half mile downstream. If they kept going straight in the direction you told them, it would take hours before they would intersect." Marcy did not keep the venom from her voice.

"I said I was sorry." Nancy turned and Blake saw her shoulders shake with what he assumed were her croc-odile tears.

Blake ignored the simpering, whiny woman. "Did you look in that direction?" he asked.

"Yes, I did. Troy and I both went, but we didn't want to get lost, either. We went a quarter mile and then searched about a mile deep. I went southwest and Troy went southeast in case they got turned around."

"Okay, well, hopefully they knew to stay put once they realized they were lost." That much Blake remembered from Boy Scouts. I've got Jack Riggs on the way, and Adam Paxton with search and rescue coming, and once they are here and the game warden and his people, they can take over, but they'll want to search in grids. Might as well start. So, let's cover the east now and save them some time. Do one mile in, turn to the left," he pointed in the direction he wanted each to take. "Take fifty paces and then make your way back. Got it?"

Troy and Marcy nodded.

"What about me?" Nancy whined.

"You can come with me or stay here in case they come back," Blake ordered.

Nancy nodded and resumed her seat on a log.

Blake noticed each had a flashlight. "Each of you take a bottle of water, too. Marcy, take the first aid kit with you. I've got mine in the car, and an extra one for Troy."

Marcy took the first aid kit Blake handed her and a bottle of water from the cooler. With one look back at Blake, Marcy nodded and put on a brave face to go search for her boys.

They were all back to the point of origin within fifteen minutes. Blake began to give directions for another attempt. As he was about to begin the next grid search, Jack arrived with lights and sirens. He kept them blaring as he swung out of his vehicle.

Jack noticed the worried expression on Blake's face as he approached him. He gave Marcy a sympathetic smile and clapped Blake on the back. "What do you need me to do?"

"I called you because…" Blake shrugged. "Well, I'm from New York City. I have not the faintest clue how to track them."

Jack grinned. "You'll learn. Let me get my gear and I'll get started. Cell and radio reception are pretty sketchy out here, but we'll stay in touch. Y'all wait on Conor t'get here."

Jack returned to the truck and pulled out a small pack. "Where'd they start and which direction did they go?"

Blake quickly caught him up to speed and explained what attempts had been made so far to locate the boys. With the next directions given, Jack turned his face to the wind. "Do your job, New York. And watch your six. I am going to search in that direction." With those parting words, Jack went off.

Marcy did not know how much time had passed. It could have been an hour, maybe two. She didn't know. She paced the campsite, calling out for her boys periodically, her voice raw from her earlier attempts at getting the boys to hear her while she was searching.

Conor had arrived shortly after Jack and he came with a squad. Blake caught him up to speed, then he and his group of volunteers set off. Conor had also brought along his wife, a woman named Erin who stayed with Marcy while the others poured over maps and set off in the directions Conor sent them.

"I know telling you not to worry won't make it happen, but Conor knows this land like no one else, Marcy. They will find your kids. Adam and Austin, is it?" Erin asked, keeping her voice calm and reassuring. The woman was trying to keep Marcy distracted.

There were eight men and four women out there looking for her kids. The thought of a dozen searchers with more on the way didn't ease her mind. The pit in her stomach gnawed at her. It wouldn't go away until she laid eyes on her boys.

Nancy had gone to wait in the car. No one cared as the volunteers dedicated themselves to finding the missing twins. Her lack of concern made little impression on Marcy at the moment, but she filed it away in the back of her mind along with her other suspicions.

Marcy went to the map Conor had laid out. Little red X's marked the pieces of land they had each searched. Not many. But they would go all night if need be, Conor promised the last time he arrived back at the base camp. Each time the volunteers came back it took them a little longer as they had to go farther into the Texas scrub.

Marcy heard feet approaching and quickly whipped around to see several of the volunteers returning. She could not hide her disappointment. She felt Erin's thin arm wrap around her and give her squeeze. "They'll find them, Marcy. I promise."

The volunteers went to the map and made more red X's and took off as others came in.

Conor announced to the group, "From now on, let's use the radios to call in the areas you have examined. It is taking too long to make the return trip. Adam…" Not Marcy's Adam, but the Adam who had come with search and rescue she thought dismally. "You coordinate and send out the locations, okay?"

"Got it!"

He gave the returning volunteers radios and the new directions. The men and women set out, not to return to base until the boys were found. Marcy's fear continued to grow as each minute ticked by.

Blake emerged from the brush. His was scratched from low-hanging branches, but his face was determined. He conversed with Adam, then made his way over to Marcy, just as she heard the most heavenly sound in the world to her.

"Mom? Mom?" came the distinct voices of her sons.

She looked in the direction of the voices. Everyone's gazes swung in that direction. Cheers resounded at the campsite.

Blake watched as the twins ran ahead of Jack. He had found them! The boys rushed to Marcy and she to them. She engulfed them in her arms and inhaled their scent. Kissing each on the head, she pulled away to look them over, like mothers do. Then two other arms wrapped around them all. Troy had just returned from a break in the search.

166

The chatter of the radios called to all the volunteers to head back in. The boys had been found.

Blake was the first to thank Jack. He had set off ahead of the others, and this was the first time Blake had seen him return. He pulled him aside to have a private word with him. Jack brushed off his words of thanks. "Just doin' m'job." He paused. "You sure you aren't too close to the situation?"

"No, Boss. I got this." Blake stared him in the eye.

Jack leaned in and glanced in Nancy's direction. "Figure out what's happening. You need help, ask. Just keep me in the loop."

"I appreciate—"

Jack cut him off. "Do your job, New York."

Gratitude swept through Blake. Jack had been out searching the whole time. He knew Jack was known in these parts as not only being an amazing sheriff, but a good tracker. Well, he sure had lived up to that reputation tonight.

Marcy, not willing to let go of her children just yet, thanked him from her family huddle on the ground. Troy called out his thanks as well. Nancy stood apart from the group, looking slightly bored and perhaps a tad guilt-ridden. She gave him a smile and tight little thank you. Jack nodded at her as his eyes narrowed.

Marcy hugged her boys tighter and watched as the man who had found them pulled Blake to the side. She would thank him later for thinking to call Jack. "Oh boy," she teased through her tears, "are you guys in trouble."

"We're sorry, Mom," Austin said as tears left dirty streaks on his face.

"So sorry, Mom. Dad." Adam repeated his brother's words.

"It's okay," she soothed. "You are okay and that is all that matters."

CHAPTER 22

"I was terrified," Marcy confessed to Jemma the next day as they spoke on the phone.

"How did Troy react?" her friend asked.

"He was as terrified as I was and relieved when the boys were found." That fact had made her reaffirm her belief that Troy was not involved in whatever devious plans Nancy may have had.

"When I heard later what happened and you hadn't shown up to the Halloween event, I was beside myself with worry."

"I'm scared, Jemma. Nancy seemed off last night. I had such a hard time not tearing into her. I know Blake doesn't have anything concrete on her, but now I am worried about Troy, too."

"I know, sweetie. He wasn't a great husband to you, but she is obviously hiding something. Where is Blake now?"

"He's working, holed up in the office. I'm home with the boys, and I keep checking the security app every couple of minutes. I am really glad to have this security system, or I don't think I would make it through the day."

"Angel is so glad he had it installed for you. We both are. But if you want, we can come over today. How are the boys?"

"No, it's not necessary for you and Angel to come over. Blake will be here later, and probably stay the night. The boys are watching a movie. I grounded them for lying to their father and to me. No video games for two weeks. I also told Troy I needed the boys with me for the next two weekends, and thankfully, he didn't give me an argument. I told him my sister was not feeling well, and I would be driving to her place the next two weekends while her husband is on a business trip."

"Good plan. I know your sister doesn't talk to Troy so there is no way for her to ruin your cover story."

"That's why I suggested we use her. I am so worried, though. I am thinking I might accept Troy's offer. If I do, maybe these accidents will stop happening."

"Marcy, I know you're afraid, but you need to stick to your guns. You don't think Troy is behind any of it, do you?"

"I don't think so, but I can't be sure. For the most part, I really don't think he is involved. He loves the boys. There's no doubt about it. But Nancy has him under some kind of spell. I don't know if these events have been coincidences or not. I need some peace of mind. Am I jumping the gun? Being too paranoid?"

"No, you're not. Blake thinks something is up and he has years of experience. Trust him."

Marcy sighed. Yes, Blake had the experience, but were his feelings for her clouding his judgment? "I do trust him. Oh God, I just don't know what to do."

Jemma didn't want Marcy to make any rash decisions. "If you say yes to Troy, how is that going to affect your future? I mean, I know you want to be safe, feel safe, but maybe you could ask Troy for a little more time. Can you stall the mediation for two weeks? Tell him your swamped with your sister being ill and once her husband is back, you can have the meeting."

"That's a thought. It will give Blake more time to investigate. Yes, I'll call my lawyer and see what he thinks. Thanks, Jemma, I will follow your suggestion."

After Marcy hung up with Jemma, she peeked in on the boys who were fully engrossed in their movie, so she headed to her office to grade papers and make some headway on her book.

She had written two chapters last week and felt proud of them. She examined the plot chart she had posted on the bulletin board above her computer. What lesson could be taught to the niece in chapter three, she mused. Don't trust a man. No. There were some you could trust. She trusted Blake. Use your head in matters of the heart. Possibly. Be aware of women using fake names. Ugh, she couldn't focus. It was a lost cause. She couldn't think about her book plot today. Not with everything happening around her.

She grabbed her phone and checked the app for what seemed like the hundredth time that day. No movement outside. No alerts. No one coming down the drive. But it had started to rain. It was barely eleven. She could make an early lunch for the boys. And maybe start preparations on the stew she planned to make for dinner. Meal prep. Yes, she could do that. Stay busy.

She pushed herself away from her desk in disgust and went into the kitchen. "Turkey or roast beef?" she called over the explosions on the television. The boys looked up a moment from their positions on opposite sides of the sofa.

"Turkey."

"Roast beef."

"With a pickle."

"And chips."

"Sweet tea, too."

"Me, too."

Marcy washed her hands in the sink and grabbed a loaf of bread. "Coming up in five minutes."

By six o'clock the rain came down in torrents. By the time Blake burst into Marcy's house, his drenched shirt clung to his skin. The fall shower was not typical for the area, but fit Marcy's mood perfectly that day. The sound of distant thunder brought back memories of the storm and tornados from four months earlier. It seemed like yesterday. She shuddered at the memory of all the people who had been hurt and families who had lost so much.

"I think I have some t-shirts that will fit." She winked at him and went to her room to retrieve one. He had stashed a few in a drawer she had cleared out for him a month ago.

"Thanks," he said, passing her in the hall and heading into the bathroom.

"Boys, can you set the table for me while I finish the salad?"

Both boys contritely did what they were told. They had watched another movie in the afternoon, and by three o'clock both were bored, they had pronounced. Several times.

"Read a book," she had snapped at them after they repeated the phrase every parent hated to hear at least half a dozen times.

"We can play Monopoly after dinner," she suggested when both looked at her like she was an alien. "I might even let you win one game." Her teasing tone evoked a rolling of their eyes.

Both moped around the house. With the rain, they couldn't even go outside. They would have to don rain jackets later to take the dogs out after they ate. The dogs would get drenched, of course, so she planned to wipe them down with several old towels she had found in the barn. Angel had probably used them with his own animals on days like these.

"Ugh, Monopoly. I don't know." Austin made a face.

"How about Clue?" Blake suggested, coming down the hall and catching the end of their conversation. He gave Marcy a quick kiss on the cheek and opened the refrigerator to grab a beer. She kept the brand he liked on stock.

"I guess," Adam whined, adding a fork and knife to each napkin he had folded. "But we are bound to lose playing against a detective."

Austin sat down at the table with a resounding plop after taking the salad bowl and placing it next to the stew Marcy had prepared for them.

Blake joined the two boys and held out the chair for Marcy to sit. When she sat, he joined them. He felt the tension in the air. Marcy and he were on edge over the current investigation. The boys over their punishment. He needed to do something to turn the day around for them all. Distract the boys and Marcy from their current bad mood.

He loved having dinner with her and the boys. He had been coming over a lot more, and they had gotten along well. Tonight was different. Everyone seemed to be in an especially foul mood. He needed to think of something to change it or they would be in for a long night. He remembered seeing a pack of balloons in Marcy's junk drawer and came up with a perfect solution.

As Marcy began to serve the food, he suggested something that might turn their night around. "Hey, how about balloon dare?"

Adam looked at him with interest. 'What's that?"

"Yeah, what's that?" repeated Austin.

"I loved this game as kid. Everyone gets two slips of paper and you write down one thing you want to know the truth about or, you know, silly stuff you want to see someone do. You fold them really small and stick them into the balloons, and then you blow them up with the paper inside."

"Okay, I am liking the sound of this," Austin said enthusiastically. "That could be fun."

"How do we know who gets which balloon?" Adam asked.

"Well, it works best if everyone has the same color of balloons. That way when it is your turn to pick you don't know if you are picking the balloon with your own slip of paper. So be careful what you write down or you have to do it or reveal a secret."

"I have a bunch of blue ones from the boys' birthday party last year," Marcy piped in. Blake's idea was a good one. The boys' moods seemed to be picking up and goodness knew she sure could use the distraction.

"Perfect. So after we write our things down and fold the slips of paper, we put them into the balloons and blow them up. Then, we can spin a bottle and whoever it points at has to pick one of the random balloons, pop it, and then do or say whatever it tells them to do."

"That sounds like fun. Yes, let's do that." Adam began to eat with more vigor. "Great stew, Mom."

"Oh boy, I already know what my dare is going to be, and, believe me, no one is going to want to pick it." Austin laughed evilly which made Marcy laugh.

Across the table from her, Marcy got Blake's attention, winked his way, and mouthed thank you. It was the first time today she felt at ease.

His smile in response brightened her spirits even more.

* * *

"Oh, my God, you look ridiculous, Mom."

The boys laughed as she walked out of her room. She had gotten a dare. She was dressed with all mismatched pieces of clothing. She wore flowered leggings and a horizontal striped blouse. She had put on two different colored socks and a huge purple bow in her hair. She had finished her ensemble with one sneaker and one cowboy boot. "Whoever wrote that down is going to pay." Not only had she to put this ridiculous ensemble together, but she wasn't allowed to take it off for the rest of the evening.

Blake laughed. She did look funny, but to him she was still beautiful. "Wow! I am so glad I did not get that one. I would have had to borrow some clothes, and well, flowers and stripes look great on you, babe, but I don't think I would have been able to ever live that down."

He had gotten one dare and one truth so far. He had been made to burp the entire alphabet, and he had to tell everyone his greatest fear. She had laughed when he said snakes. "Boy, oh boy, did you pick the wrong state to move to if you are afraid of snakes."

He liked seeing her laugh. "I hate them. I have been lucky so far. Just the thought of them makes me get the cold sweats."

"Well, you better get yourself a jacket and keep your eyes peeled on the ground. We see them all the time around here, don't we Adam?" Austin teased and winked at his brother.

"Oh yes, sir. All the time." The boys were not afraid of snakes in the least. Troy had taught them which ones to avoid.

Each of the boys had pulled a truth so far. Adam had to reveal his secret crush. He turned five shades of purple but confessed he had a crush on a girl in tenth grade named Tiffany. Austin had to confess the worst thing he'd done in school, and he had admitted to putting packets of ketchup on the toilet seat in middle school. Marcy remembered it well. She had been called to the school over quite a few pranks. She was glad the boys seemed past the pranking stage, well, except for their most recent stunt that had landed them punished for the next two weeks. Austin had been caught and grounded for the ketchup incident, too.

There were three balloons left. Marcy spun the bottle and it pointed to Adam. "Uh-oh," she tormented her son. "There are two dares and one truth left, what are you going to get?" Her dare was still in one of the balloons, and it was a doozy.

Adam nervously peered at the three remaining balloons. He made his choice, then using the tip of a pen, popped it. The dogs jumped from their spots on the sofa and barked like they had done for each balloon busted so far. Blake, once again, made quick work of picking up the pieces so they didn't swallow any. Adam slowly unfolded the slip of paper. "Dang it! I got mine. I really wanted to see Blake get this one."

Blake eyed Adam suspiciously. "Oh, really, now, what did you have in mind for me?"

Adam slipped the paper into his pocket and began

to dance around the room for an entire minute pretending to be a gorilla. Marcy laughed so hard she almost cried.

"I see how it is. Make a monkey out of me. I will get you back next time we play."

There were two balloons left. Adam spun the bottle, and Marcy scooted away when it looked like it would land on her again. She got lucky, and the bottle spun to Austin. "Mine have been picked already, and I know I gotta fifty-fifty chance of not having to do some crazy dare." He put his hands before him in mock prayer, then plucked a balloon without any further hesitation. He popped it and found the slip of paper on the floor. "Oh no. I got the last dare. Oh brother. This is re-donk-u-lous!" He used one of his favorite new words.

"What does it say?" Adam asked. Marcy already knew. It was the dare she had written on the slip.

"I have to sing a love song to Champ and Chewie. With *feeling*!" Everyone laughed. Marcy couldn't keep a straight face when Austin gave her the evil eye. "I know you wrote this, Mom."

She nodded as Austin sat before the dogs, made a joke out of clearing his voice, and belted out "I Will Always Love You" by Whitney Houston to Champ and Chewie. He was so bad but so into it the dogs started howling which sent them all into another fit of giggles.

Though Austin butchered the lyrics, he kept singing and made up the lyrics he didn't know as he went along. It made the performance funnier. He sang until Chewie buried his head under the pillow and Champ trotted out of the room in disgust. The others clapped for him.

"Encore, encore!" Adam called.

"Please, no," Marcy cried, wiping the tears from her eyes.

"I gotta agree with your mom on that one. Stick to baseball, kid."

"Okay, well, let me spin that thing and see who gets the last balloon," Austin said and took his spot to the right of Marcy. The bottle spun wildly and eventually landed on Blake.

"No fair, I have already done two, your mom should have to answer this one," he said, reaching for the balloon. His question was inside, and he knew what his answer was to it, but he really wanted to hear Marcy's answer. He looked at Marcy, dared her with a look to take the balloon for him. "Plus, I did write the question, so I already know my answer."

Marcy gave Blake a suspicious look, but then accepted the challenge. "Fine, give it to me." He handed it to her, she cupped the balloon between her knees and popped it with the pen that Adam handed her. She snatched the slip of paper from Blake who picked it up off the rug. Her eyes misted over when she saw the question and she looked into Blake's eyes. His eyes were filled with the answer to the question he had asked. She knew what he would say without his even saying a word. It was in his eyes, in his actions, in everything he did for her. His protectiveness, his worry, his time and patience, and his willingness to immerse himself in her life. Marcy quickly stuffed the slip of paper into a pocket on her flowered leggings. "You. My answer is you."

"Hey, no fair, what was the question, Mom?"

Marcy froze. She felt strange saying it in front of her children. It was too soon, but they were definitely headed in the right direction. Fortunately, Blake stepped in to save her.

"It said, 'Who is a better cook, Blake or Marcy'?"

"Oh, man, that was a lame question," Austin declared, beginning to pick up the bits of balloon and putting the cushions back onto the sofa they had been sitting on.

"Plus, everyone likes other people's cooking better than their own," Adam added, helping his brother to tidy up without being asked. "Especially if they don't have to do it."

"That's true," Marcy agreed. "I really do love it when someone cooks for me once in a while. I still say my hamburgers are better than his. But I will give him this because that pasta the other night was a little bit of heaven."

"Well, I do make great Italian food," Blake agreed, "but if I had gotten that question, I would have said you, too, Marcy. You." His word was the answer she had seen in his eyes, the answer to the real question he had asked.

What kind of person would you want to marry in the future?

Now, they both knew each other's answer, and they both knew they were in it for the long haul.

CHAPTER 23

By mid-November, Marcy felt frantic. Her rescheduled mediation was in a few days, and to top it off, Troy had asked to have the kids for Thanksgiving. He was going to his parents' house and wanted them with him when he introduced Nancy to his folks. She didn't know how she was going to get out of it.

"Blake has come up with nothing yet," Marcy complained to Jemma. "He even went to North Carolina and the family there said Nancy was in Texas, and they had not seen her in ten years. The picture he showed them could be her one cousin said, and Blake had been told by a distant uncle that her father had received some pretty hefty bills from a plastic surgeon."

"Well, then, maybe you don't have to worry about her."

"No, Jemma. I'm still worried. It doesn't explain how two people who are wanted for questioning in the case of that missing artist who turned up dead were driving her car."

"I know. It's suspicious. And Blake can't ask her without blowing his investigation, can he?"

"Afraid not."

Marcy knew Jemma was worried about her. Though things were going great with Blake, Jemma noticed Marcy was as jumpy as a cat in a room full of rockers when he wasn't around. "What does Blake say?"

"Keep being cautious. Thank goodness he comes over almost every night. I don't sleep well unless he is here. The boys have been okay with it, though he usually leaves before they are up."

"Well," Jemma lightened her tone. "Focus on that. On him."

Marcy had told her about the balloon game. Jemma knew she was falling hard for Blake, even if she wouldn't say the words.

Still anxious, Marcy needed an outing to get her mind off things. "Hey, how about coming with me today for some shopping therapy? I need to go to San Antonio, but before I do, I have to stop by Gant Meadows' place and pick up a belt buckle I commissioned for Angel. His work is amazing," Jemma suggested.

"Gant Meadows, the recluse? The one the locals call G-man?"

"Yeah. He inherited the property from his grandfather a few years back and has done a lot of work on it. He seems a bit odd, I know, but Jack likes him. He keeps to himself, but word has gotten out about the work he does. I checked the place out a few weeks ago. He sells stuff he makes, beautiful jewelry, knives, swords, and all kinds of things, right on his property, so he doesn't have to go anywhere. It's pretty cool when you catch him working, too. He is a real master of the forge."

"I guess that would be fun. I haven't even thought about Christmas shopping yet." It was six weeks away, and she hadn't purchased a thing yet. "The boys planned to go fishing with Blake today, and I don't mind bowing out for some retail therapy."

"Have they left yet?"

"No."

"Ooo, Angel would love to go. I'll pick you up in an hour. The boys can make a day of it, and we can hang for some girl time and shopping!"

"You made my day."

When Jemma and Marcy hopped out of Angel's truck, they heard Gant Meadows working in his forge. The clang of the man's hammer hitting the metal on the anvil sounded almost relaxing, strangely enough. The large man was focused on the task at hand, and he barely glanced up when they went inside the little shop. He just continued to wield his hammer.

"Be with you in a minute," he said, the words not making him miss a strike. So focused was he, the rhythm of his motions did not falter on the blade he fashioned. Gant made her think of Wayland the Smith from *Beowulf*, a Dark Ages character who crafted armor and weapons for a cruel king. He finally managed to create a magical winged cloak to escape his imprisonment. Even his appearance seemed to fit a man who had been plucked from ancient times. He was rough and dark and broad and brooding. Watching him work was like stepping into another world.

"Oh, this would be perfect for Blake." Jemma plucked an item on display from a shelf.

Distracted, Marcy glanced away from Gant to see what Jemma held in her hand. It was an ornately crafted knot shield with a silver overlay. "Oh my. It's nice. The craftmanship is amazing. It's also a knot shield which is a symbol of protection, isn't it?" Blake was working so hard to keep her safe. Her protector. "I think I'll buy it. It will be the perfect Christmas present."

"Yes, I'm sure Blake will love it. Plus, we definitely need to *Texas* that guy up." Jemma handed the item to Marcy who placed it delicately on the counter as they waited for Gant to finish. He wasn't too much longer, but Jemma picked out a few more pieces to purchase, some earrings for her cousin, Bella, and matching ones for herself.

"I have your buckle right under here, Mrs. Murphy," Gant interjected, not making eye contact with either of them as he came into the room wiping his hands on his apron. Sweat trickled down his brow, and he swiped at it with one massive forearm before snatching an item already boxed up from underneath the counter.

"Please add these two sets of earrings."

"Huh," Gant growled, looking at what Jemma placed on the counter. "Two hundred fifty for the buckle, fifty for each set of earrings. That okay?"

Jemma nodded and handed four crisp one hundred dollar bills to Gant. He gave her fifty back.

"And you want that buckle, Mrs. Fields, isn't it? Or your maiden name again?"

"Marcy," she said, swallowing hard. Even the town recluse knew she was getting divorced. Two hundred and fifty for Jemma's buckle for Angel. She hoped the one she had picked out wasn't much more. She only had three hundred on her. She didn't think the man took credit cards. "And, um, yes. How much is it?"

Gant eyed the woman before him. He had heard about her. Going through rough times. Two growing boys. He didn't socialize much, but he heard a lot when he went out. He listened. "A hundred and fifty." He had intended to sell it for three hundred, but the woman had broken out in a cold sweat when she heard the prices he quoted to Jemma. The straight lines on the knot shield had been a bitch to make. But her look of relief made his discount worth it. He watched as her hands shook while she counted out the money.

Gant took the cash and put the silver buckle in a box with a cleaning cloth and a little piece of paper that explained how to keep it looking like new. Then he tossed it in a bigger bag and threw in two little paper envelopes with forged fish hooks. "Fish hooks for the boys. No charge, ma'am."

"Oh my, thank you, Mr. Meadows."

"Gant, or G-man is fine."

"Mr. ... I mean Gant. May I use your restroom?" The trip to San Antonio wasn't too long of a ride, but she had forgotten to go before leaving her house and didn't want to make Jemma have to stop along the way.

Gant Meadows' face drew a blank. He stared at her for a moment like she had two heads, but then nodded. "The door is open. Up the stairs and to the left," he indicated with a chin tilt. "I must be getting back to my work. Have a good day." Without another word, he turned on his booted heel, picked up his hammer, and went back into the forge.

Marcy and Jemma exchanged stark glances and scurried out of the shop, trying to contain their laughter. They managed to do so until they got into the old Meadows' farmhouse. Then they let it out.

"Oh, my goodness, did you *see* how he looked at you when you asked to use his bathroom?"

"I thought he was going to ask for the buckle back *and* the fish hooks."

Jemma followed Marcy up the stairs of the surprisingly clean house for a single man who looked like he spent most of his time standing in front of a furnace. She was under strict orders by Blake not to let Marcy out of her sight. "That was nice of him, though. I think he undercharged on that buckle, too."

"I think so as well. Very nice of him. He looks so intimidating, but maybe he is all gruff on the outside, and just a big softie on the inside," Marcy observed, going up the last few stairs.

"Well, from what I hear," Jemma said as Marcy reached for the knob on the door to the bathroom, "the guy has been here four years and other than shopping at the food mart and getting his supplies, he never leaves the place. A real loner, that one."

"OMG!" Marcy cried the moment she opened the door. She pointed at the shower rod. "What is that?"

Jemma looked twice at the lacy thing hanging off the shower curtain rod, back at Marcy, and then at the lacy thing again. She started to laugh. "It's a bra!"

Marcy laughed, too. "I thought you said he never gets out? Move, please. I really gotta go now." Marcy began to unfasten her pants, and Jemma turned to give her some privacy.

"Maybe, OMG," Jemma giggled, "maybe…maybe," she couldn't get the words out, "maybe he's a cross dresser."

"Holy shit!" Marcy laughed hard at the thought of the huge man dressed as a woman. "No way. Not him."

"How do we explain the bra then?" Jemma pointed at the object.

"We don't," Marcy replied, flushing, then pulling up her pants. "We never speak of it again, and we never mention this to anyone." She washed her hands in the basin. "That guy works in a forge. He seems kind enough, but he has a big hammer, and we just saw with our own eyes he knows how to use it."

Jemma laughed as Marcy finished up, but her comments had her sides hurting. "You know, I better go, too, 'cuz, I don't think I can make it to San Antonio either now."

They switched places.

Marcy turned for Jemma. But soon she was in

another fit of hysterics when Jemma asked, "How does he get that wee, itty-bitty thing around his torso?"

"Jemma, stop!" Marcy cried.

"It can't be bigger than a 34 C. It's impossible."

"Stop."

CHAPTER 24

Marcy left the mediation meeting feeling defeated. Done.

Troy, on the other hand, was elated. She had made the decision, moments before, to accept his terrible offer. The past few weeks had been so stressful for her. She felt as if someone were watching her. Jumpy and anxious, she knew the kids at school and her own boys noticed the change in her. At least Troy was gracious enough to agree to pay her attorney's fees from the sale of the house. Her lawyer had insisted upon it before he would allow her to accept the pitiful offer.

Troy told her he would put the house in Banderas on the market the next day. And with the way real estate was moving in that area, they should be able to sell the house before the end of the month.

Blake was home with the boys when she got there. He had gotten off work early so he could pick them up from baseball conditioning for her. The boys were doing their homework when she arrived. Blake met her on the porch, carrying two bottles of beer.

"Thought you could use one today." Blake offered her a bottle and she accepted it. She wasn't a beer drinker, but today, she really wanted it.

"I do. Thank you." He uncapped it for her and waited while she took a long, cool sip.

"So, what happened?" he asked after a moment of silence. He knew she was hurting. No matter what she had decided to do, he supported her. But it was hard going through a divorce even when both parties wanted it. He knew that firsthand.

Marcy leaned against one of the railings and sighed. "I...I relented. I accepted his measly offer. I just wanted to be done with it. We go before a judge possibly this week or early next week to make it official."

Blake understood her choice. He knew her fear had made her capitulate more than anything else. She may have continued to fight except for a dark cloud of suspicion hanging over Nancy. "You did?"

"Yup. I did. The lawyers are drawing up the papers, and we only need to sign them in front of the judge."

"I'm sorry, babe." He put his beer down on the railing and took hers and set it next to his own. Then he pulled her into his arms for a full body hug. His arms might comfort her, he hoped.

Marcy felt some of her tension and worry over her future dissipate in Blake's arms. With him in her life, she would eventually feel safe. Right now, she still felt uncertain. Once Blake finished his investigation, she would start a new life with him. Money wasn't all that important, she told herself. She could pay the bills and keep a roof over her children's heads. That was the most important thing to her. They would find their happiness in each other.

"Want to sit out here for a while and talk about it?" Blake offered.

She shrugged, but said, "Sure." The boys were still doing their homework, so now was as good a time as any to decompress. She took a seat on one of the two rockers and he sat next to her. "You know, I'm not sad about the divorce. Or even the settlement. Not really. I have been making it work for months now. I can get by. We will survive. It's just disappointment in Troy eating away at me. It makes me mad he really thinks or thought so little of me. My value and contribution to our marriage. That hurts."

"I can promise you I will never do that." She looked into his eyes and knew he was an honest man. To the core. He was dependable, loyal, and loving. She had been so incredibly lucky to have found him.

Marcy smiled. "I know. You're definitely one of the good ones. I think I will keep you around."

Her words were meant to tease, to lighten the mood. However, they caused Blake's heart to slam into his chest. Pure, unadulterated love swept through him. He'd fallen in love with Marcy quite some time ago but kept his feelings to himself. He swallowed the heavy lump in his throat. He couldn't allow another day to pass without telling Marcy how he felt about her. "You know I love you, Marcy. I haven't said it yet, but you know I do, right?"

Marcy put her bottle down once more as did he when he saw her intention. She settled in his lap, his arms already open to accept her. "You know I love you, too, right? I'm not saying it because you did first."

"I do. I believe you. You're an amazing woman, Marcy. I thank the stars every day I made the decision to move to Texas each time I think of you." His passionate declaration and the tenor of his voice thrilled Marcy. She didn't think she would ever forget this moment.

She bent toward him. Their mouths met in a tender kiss sealing their love.

"Tomorrow I want to go horseback riding," Marcy announced at dinner. They had all helped to make homemade pizza. "You guys game?"

Blake made a face. He rubbed his backside which made the boys laugh. "I dunno 'bout that. Last time we went riding, I was sore for a week."

"But you did good, New York," Adam teased Blake. They had heard Jack Riggs call him that the other day when they ran into him in town. The boys thought it was funny and had occasionally started using it. "Plus, Mom loves horses, so if you are gonna stick with her, it's just something you gotta do to keep the lady happy."

"Oh, is that so?" Blake asked, throwing a piece of pepperoni at Adam.

"Mom goes fishing with us, so it's only fair," Austin stated matter-of-factly.

"Wait! What? She doesn't like fishing?" Blake looked aghast.

"Hates it!" both boys said in unison.

"Yes, I do. It's true." Marcy said, taking a bite of her delicious slice. "But I do love making pizza with you."

They had been riding for over an hour. Pops let them come out to his ranch and ride some of his horses. Blake had been bonding with Pops through his work with the TVFD. He enjoyed working with the other guys and gals of the TVFD. Jack had been right about that. Volunteer there and soon you will know practically everyone in the vicinity.

"I must say, I love Texas, and I think I'm getting used to riding these horses." Blake turned the mare he was riding like a pro down the path winding around Pop's large ranch. The others followed his lead.

"I think you are getting better," Adam said. "You are holding the reins right, and you're keeping a good seat." Both boys had learned to ride from Marcy. She had grown up on a ranch and had several of her own horses. But after she married and her folks sold their place, she had missed it terribly. Pops was always kind enough to let people come out to his stables and ride his horses.

"Definitely," Marcy agreed. "You won't be as sore. I promise."

"How was baseball practice yesterday?" Blake asked. Conditioning after school had now officially become practice. He had been spending a lot of time with them and had given them a few tips these last few weeks. He also knew the boys were pretty excited to be playing their first game for the high school. It was only a pre-season game since baseball didn't officially start until February, but the local coaches always arranged a few games between local schools so the players got used to playing against other teams. It helped them to ease into the upcoming schedule. Currently, Adam would be starting as pitcher and Austin would be playing shortstop.

"It went great. Coach was really impressed with the way I have been catching those grounders. He says I am good enough to play varsity next year." Blake believed it. The kid was fast, had a great arm for long distance, and his reaction time was astounding. He was a natural.

"That's great. And what about your pitching, Adam? What is the coach saying about you?"

"Same thing. Impressed all the way around. He told me to tell you whatever that Blake Levine fellow from New York is doing with you boys to keep it up. He said next year he wants you to be an assistant coach if you got some spare time. Coach Watkins is retiring at the end of the season."

"Absolutely. Yeah. I'll go talk to him. I mean I can't do it every day, not with my day job, but we can definitely work something out. I can probably come out to the field two, maybe three. times a week. I'll talk to him."

Watching and listening to her boys and Blake filled

Marcy with happiness. Her boys were learning so much from him. On their first official date, he had told her he had always thought about coaching. He saw it as an opportunity to get involved with young boys who needed a role model. It wasn't just about teaching them the game, but teaching them how to be a team player and how to be a man. He was a natural with kids.

"Even Dad and Uncle Corey were impressed. They came out to our practice yesterday."

"Uncle Corey?" Marcy asked. Troy didn't have a brother.

Blake pulled up short on his reins and his gentle mare gave a little whinny of surprise. All three of them stopped their horses behind him on the narrow path. He turned to look at the twins. "Who is Uncle Corey?" He knew Troy was an only child. Marcy had one sister. And according to his records, Nancy had only one sibling, too, a sister who was quite a bit younger than she.

Adam looked startled. "Um, well, it's Nancy's brother. He came into town this week. Seems okay. He is staying with them for a few weeks. He came out for the holidays."

Marcy looked at Blake sideways. He must be thinking the same thing she was. He had told her a few weeks earlier Nancy Reeves had just one younger sister in North Carolina and they weren't close at all. Nancy was a black sheep sent to live in exile from her blue-blooded family for an embarrassing affair with a close friend of her father's.

Blake's blood ran cold, but he didn't want to scare

the boys or Marcy. The name Corey had struck a nerve. All the pieces of the puzzle were now beginning to fall into place. He knew Marcy was about to ask the question written all over her face, so he stopped her with one look. "That's nice she has her brother in town. Hey, you getting hungry?" At the boys' nod and her shrug, he continued, "Let's call it day and head back in. I forgot I needed to do something at the office. Won't take long. You guys can come with me, for a bit, or perhaps, I can find someone to take you over to the cantina for some burritos while I finish up what I forgot to do."

"Bur-rito! Bur-rito!" chanted Austin who was always hungry. His brother joined in. That one word was a sure-fire bet to distract her sons, and Blake knew it. What had he figured out? From the expression on his face when the boys weren't looking, she knew it wasn't good.

Marcy nodded at Blake and knew something had finally clicked.

* * *

Blake resisted putting the metal to the pedal on the drive into Banderas. He didn't want the kids to be aware of his and Marcy's concern. Thankfully, she picked up the slack with the boys, peppering them with questions about an upcoming school event while he was deep in thought.

One. Corey was the name used by Noreen Hall's brother. Noreen was the wife of the artist found murdered in the desert. Two. Nancy Reeves did not have a brother. Just a sister eight years younger she hadn't seen in ten years. Three. Corey was seen driving Nancy Reeves' stolen car in Oregon. Four. Blake had initially suspected, but hadn't been able to prove, that this Nancy was an imposter. What was the connection between the three people? It was right there in front of him. He just had to put two and two together. Or in this case three.

He knew he was getting close. Think, he told himself. Go over the pieces one more time. The cousin, the only person who would speak to him in North Carolina, could barely remember Nancy. She was closer in age to the younger sister. The sister, Sarah, had been only eight the last time she had seen her wild sister, Nancy. Their mother had died, and the father wanted nothing to do with his daughter who had slept with his closest friend, a senator who was forced to resign from office. Her actions in the revelation of the affair had been humiliating to the senator and his wife, and her own mother's early demise of a heart attack. Daddy Reeves wouldn't even take his call. He told his secretary to tell him that he would pay Nancy's medical bills and she would receive a monthly allowance of five thousand dollars if she stayed out of trouble and never returned to North Carolina. If she broke those two simple rules, she would be cut off.

What was he missing? Had it been Nancy in that car or Noreen? Why had she reported the car stolen? Money for a new one from daddy? A fight with Corey? How did Corey know both Nancy and Noreen? Being both of their brothers was clearly impossible. Then it him like a bolt of lightning out of the blue. He wasn't a brother to either of them. That was a ruse. He was their patsy or their lover. Which one? Was he the guy who did their dirty work? Or the mastermind? But not to both of them. Only one of them. It clicked. Finally. Blake was almost certain Nancy and Noreen were the same person. The changes over the years. The photographs with her face hidden while married to the artist. The phone call he would make once at the station would provide the answer he needed.

But which name was the real one? Nancy. At first, he thought that was the phony name because he started with Noreen. But it was actually the other way around. He had not been able to prove Nancy wasn't real. So, Noreen had to be a false identity. The appearance thing had tripped him up, though. But he would be able to check on that, too. All three looked similar, but not like the same person. There were subtle differences, differences easily created with plastic surgery, botox injections, and eye lifts. Daddy Reeves paid his daughter's medical bills. What type of medical bills would a seemingly healthy and fit twenty-seven-year-old woman need? A vain one might get something done or several things done. He'd need a warrant for her medical records. Another call he needed to make. The noose was tightening.

He gave Marcy a sideways glance. The boys were watching a video on their phone. They had their headphone on.

"I think I have this figured out. I will tell you as

soon as we get to the office. I'll have one of the other deputies take the boys. You hold back, okay?"

Marcy agreed, but her stomach rolled. She knew the boys mentioning an Uncle Corey had triggered something for Blake. She was glad they were a few minutes away from the station. She prayed this nightmare would be over soon.

CHAPTER 25

When they got to the station, Blake was relieved to see Rodriguez was still there. Blake pulled him to the side.

"Hey, buddy. I need a favor. Think you can take the boys for me down to the cantina for some burritos? I know it's a huge favor, but I need about an hour. It's huge. I am about to blow a case wide open, and Marcy and I really don't want to have the kids bored or listening in, if you know what I mean. I wouldn't ask, but it's important."

"Sure, man. This about the murder-for-hire thing?"

"It might be related. I haven't made the connection yet, but it definitely looks like I am getting close to solving that cold case."

"Sure, you got it."

"I owe you, man."

Rodriguez fist-bumped Blake. "Hey, guys, you ready to get some burritos? I am a chimichanga man myself."

"Yes, sir. We are always ready for burritos."

"Be good, boys. Deputy Rodriguez will bring you

back here in about an hour," Marcy called after the retreating figures.

"No worries, Marcy. I got two of my own, so I know what to expect," Rodriguez assured her. To Adam and Austin he said, "You guys go to school with Julio, right?"

"Yes, sir. He's on the baseball team with us," Marcy heard Adam say as they left the building.

The moment the door closed she turned to Blake, "What's going on? What did you figure out?"

"Come to my desk. I want to show you something." Marcy followed him to his desk in his small office. Most of the guys on the shift were out or working quietly at their desks. In the corner of the room, she noticed a striking woman. She was tall, curvy, and had beautiful, short, curly chestnut-colored hair. She sat in front of a computer with files stacked beside her. She nodded at Marcy and Blake as they took a seat near her.

"Hi, Amanda."

"Hey, Blake. I didn't think you were working today."

"I'm wasn't, but now I am. You know how it goes."

"Sure do."

"This is my girlfriend, Marcy Fields. Marcy, this is Amanda Redgrave, FBI. She is working a case in the area."

"Nice to meet you," Amanda said from behind her loaner desk. "But you go right ahead, Blake. Don't mind me over here."

He nodded and pulled a chair next to his desk for Marcy to sit. Then after she did, he sat and unlocked his drawer and pulled out several files. "Okay. Marcy, this is what I want you to look at." He opened the file on the artist. He showed her the flyer of the woman with Cole Lansing. It wasn't a great photo and the woman wore big dark glasses. "So, whom does this woman look like?" he asked.

"Well, she kind of looks like Nancy, but her lips are fuller. Eyebrows are closer together, too. She isn't as well-endowed as Nancy, either."

"But similar enough to pass for family, right?"

"I guess, but I don't really see much of her face. The cheekbones look the same, though."

"Now look at this photo." He showed her the driver's license photo of Nancy Reeves when she was just seventeen from the state of North Carolina.

"Younger, a little softer looking than Nancy. She actually looks more like Noreen."

"Exactly. But I think they are all pictures of Nancy at different stages in her life. They're different because of plastic surgery."

Marcy stared at the two images. It was possible. The young girl, the young bride, and Nancy. Could it be?

"I have to make a call to confirm this. Give me one minute." He picked up the receiver. "Yes, this is Deputy Levine, Banderas Sheriff's Office, Texas."

Marcy could not hear what was said on the other end of the line. She put her hands in her lap and tried to stop them from shaking. What did this all mean?

"Yes, I know he won't speak with me, but I just need one piece of information from you. I was told that Mr. Reeves continues to pay his daughter's medical expenses. It struck me as odd since she is quite young and the family must provide her with medical insurance. So, what I need to know is if Mr. Reeves has paid for his daughter to have work done with a plastic surgeon." He paused. "Sir, if I do not get an answer, I will have no choice but to get a warrant for Mr. Reeves' personal financial records. That would become public knowledge since I would have to file in his county. So, if you could please ask Mr. Reeves for the name of the plastic surgeon, we can quickly end this call. Thank you." He held his hand over the receiver. To Marcy, Blake said, "He put me on hold."

"Her father's secretary?"

He nodded his head. "Thank you, sir. Dr. Sheffield. Got it." He hung up. His eyes filled with excitement. "The pieces are falling into place." Plastic surgeons often kept before and after photos.

"Please explain it to me. I am afraid I'm still a bit confused."

"Okay, so here is my theory. Nancy Reeves, who has a relationship with an older man, leaves North Carolina in disgrace. She attends the University of Austin. She meets a guy, I am thinking this is Corey Hall aka Charles and Carl, and they get together. College is fun. She parties and spends her money and has a taste for finer things. But when college is over, what will she do? She can't go home, the guy she is with isn't rich like her dad, or the senator, but he is easy to control and does her bidding. But the money doesn't go far when she is footing the bill for two. At some point, Nancy meets an artist, a well-to-do, up and coming artist. But she uses an alias. Noreen Hall. The artist is twice her age, doesn't have a family, so a plan is hatched.

"They marry, then he disappears without a trace. She and her lover live well for a few years spending the artist's money, her inheritance. But then the man's body is discovered and people start asking questions and looking too closely. So, Noreen Lansing disappears with her 'brother'."

He used air quotes when he said the word *brother*. "They go to Oregon. Her friend Lisa let it slip that Corey revealed he was from Oregon. I found the arrest record there for a Charles Hall driving Nancy Reeves' car. He gets pulled over for reckless driving because they are having an argument over what they have done. Maybe Corey wants out, but Nancy won't let him leave. Or maybe he is abusive and he hits her. I don't know. But she stays. Maybe one of them wants to do it again, but the other doesn't want to, so they go their separate ways for a while. She gets plastic surgery to change her appearance or fix it. I'm not sure. But anyhow, they cool their heels in Oregon or another state for three years, but money is tight, then they find their way back to Texas. This is when Nancy meets Troy. Maybe she is leaving the hospital and she catches his eye."

"That sounds about right. His eye was easy to catch."

Blake gives her a sympathetic smile. "Sorry, but the cheating doctor doesn't tell her he is a married man.

Nancy and Corey aka Charles concoct a plan to try again."

"But I am in the way," Marcy guesses.

"Yes, you and the boys. He is worth a lot, but not with a wife and kids in the picture. Your husband has properties, investments, and she knows they are tied to you unless he gets the divorce first."

"The accidents, the burglary, the boys getting lost. You don't think those were all coincidences. You think Nancy was behind it all."

"Yes, she and this Corey fellow she is trying to pass off as her brother. The MO didn't change from Noreen to Nancy. They weren't careful and used the same name."

"Probably couldn't keep it straight."

"Probably, but she used the name Danielle with the bikers, so I think Corey is or was waffling. Maybe he didn't want to hurt a woman or kids, but he conveniently shows up when you agree to the conditions of the divorce."

"Oh, my goodness, she is going after Troy." Marcy, however angry she was with the man, didn't wish him ill will.

"Not if I can stop it. Give me one second." He picked up his phone again. "Logan, yes, I need a warrant for a Dr. Sheffield. The suspect, Nancy Reeves. Yes, murder, attempted murder, and murder-for-hire," he outlined into the phone. "Please get to the judge and fax me the warrant. I want her medical records and any photos the doctor has in his files. I can run down to

San Antonio myself to get the records. Thank you. I'll owe you one."

"Will this be enough to put her away?" Marcy asked, afraid of his answer.

"It's a lot of circumstantial stuff. Enough for an arrest at the very least. In a trial, I am not sure. I'm afraid we will have to get one of them to crack, but we have to act fast."

"Excuse me," Amanda interrupted from a dozen feet away. "I really didn't mean to eavesdrop. This case sounds great on paper, but Blake is right. It's all circumstantial. Do you have any DNA on the artist? DNA of Noreen to compare to Nancy? Or just grainy photos and great detective work?"

"I can get them to crack. I have to," Blake replied, convincingly.

"May I make a suggestion?" Amanda approached the desk.

"I'm listening."

"You might not like what I am going to say, but if you really want to take these bad guys down, and they sure sound bad as hell, what about doing a sting?"

"A sting?" Blake asked, sitting up straighter.

"You said she tried to hire a biker to off Marcy."

"A couple of times."

"Let me warn you. This is the part you are not gonna like. If Marcy calls Troy and tells him she's changed her mind and won't sign the divorce agreement, he will flip. So will Nancy. Corey will run scared and she will need someone to take care of Marcy fast. This time, instead of waiting for one of the local MCs to call you with a tip, or worse acting on it, you put a plant in Nancy's path. Someone who announces he needs cash fast. She won't be able to resist."

"Isn't that entrapment?" Marcy asked.

Amanda continued, "No. Not if she pays the guy and proceeds with the plan. She will go down for attempted murder and Corey will be a conspirator. With possible threats of life in jail or worse, the death penalty, they turn on each other and you get a confession on your cold case."

"I don't know about this. Marcy would have to…. No. I can't ask her..."

"Can't ask me to do what?" Marcy asked, turning to him.

Blake looked her in the eyes, watched the rise and fall of her chest. Her hands shook. "I can't ask you to pretend to be dead. We'd have to stage your murder, have our decoy bring her evidence to ensure she gets the maximum. Look, Marcy, I can't do it. You have been on edge for three weeks. You're shaking like a leaf now."

What he said was true, but she would do anything to bring closure to this situation. "I can and most certainly will do it," Marcy declared vehemently. "I'm shaking and scared because that woman is out there and has made not one, not two, but three attempts on my, or my children's lives, and she plans on killing my ex-husband and the father of my children for his money."

Blake couldn't believe it. Marcy was the strongest woman he knew. Troy had been a fool to let her go. He knew he could not convince her to stand by and do nothing. "If you are sure."

"Hell, yes. I'm sure and the sooner the better."

"Okay, let me bring in Jack and give him the information. And we can get this ball rolling." Once more Blake picked up his phone and made the call to Jack Riggs.

CHAPTER 26

Blake let Marcy take the boys home using his vehicle. He promised to come home as soon as he could and would have one of the other deputies give him a lift, but he needed Jack Riggs' approval for the sting operation. Amanda promised to advise and help oversee the operation.

Marcy had been home for over two hours when Blake finally arrived. By that time the boys had already eaten and were ensconced in Austin's bedroom playing video games with their friends online.

Blake hadn't eaten so she warmed up some leftovers for him in case he was hungry when he arrived. "Thank you," he said. "I am starving."

Marcy sat beside him with a cup of coffee in her hands. Decaf, she was already on edge enough as it was. "So, what happened?"

"Well, Jack approved the plan and we are a go. Amanda called in a contact from Houston and he will be here tomorrow. He will serve as the decoy, and we will put him in Nancy's path."

"Tomorrow?"

"Yes. Jack thinks we need to act fast on this. So, tomorrow I will drive the boys into school, and I think you should stay home. We will have the resource officer keep a close eye on the boys. You will call Troy when I get back and let him know you have changed your mind about the settlement. You think it is too little and frankly insulting. You will need to play it up so he goes straight to Nancy with the information. Also, let him know the boys are having a sleepover at their friend's house, but don't say where. We don't want Nancy looking for them first. We want her to come after you. We will have a tail on her, so when and if, fingers crossed she heads out to a bar, we can get our decoy in place. We know a few places both in Banderas and Tarpley where she goes, and we will have another decoy in San Antonio in case she goes to the place she frequents there. But a lot of the bikers hang out in the rural areas."

"What happens then?" Marcy asked.

"Our decoy will come into the place where she is and make a ruckus. He will announce near her that he is desperate for cash. And that will hopefully be enough to convince her to approach. If she makes an offer, he will say he wants some cash up front and the rest after. Money has to exchange hands. The more the better. It means she is dead serious. Premeditated murder means she and Corey get a stiffer sentence."

"What if Corey isn't involved? Will he get off?"

"No. He is an accomplice. We will threaten him with the max, but try to get him to turn on Nancy for a reduced sentence for testifying against her. You don't have to worry; he will be going away, too, for a very long time."

"Okay." She still looked nervous, and he reached over to grab her hand. "You sure you are okay about this? I mean we can keep digging and see what we can find that way."

"No. I need this to be over. This shadow has been hanging over my head too long, plus, even though Troy is my ex, he deserves better than this. I can't risk the boys losing their father."

He understood. "Okay, well, if you are sure. The next step after money is exchanged is we fake your death. We have a makeup artist coming in to help us."

"What will that entail?" Marcy asked, but shuddered at the thought. She knew it would be gruesome.

"We make it look like you struggled a bit. Some bruises, cuts, scrapes. Dirty up your clothing. Make your skin pale."

"Okay, I can handle that."

"That's not all. We are going to have to dig a hole somewhere on the property and put you in it. Tied up. Take pictures of you here in the house and in the grave."

It was worse than she thought. Marcy wanted to heave at the mental picture he created for her, but she had to do this. For her, the boys, and Troy. Nancy had to be stopped. "What about the boys? They can't be here when this happens. It will be too much."

"Yes, I thought of that, too. I have asked Jemma and Angel to take them for the night. Jemma will have them skip baseball practice and tell them you are not feeling well and went to the doctor. I told her to tell them you had an allergic reaction so they don't worry too much. However, it will be all over the news after the arrests have been made, so we will have to tell them everything. It's better if they hear it from you rather than their friends."

"Yes. Of course."

Blake finished his meal and pushed his plate away. He rose to his feet and pulled Marcy to him. He held her in his arms. "Tomorrow," he promised. "This will all be over tomorrow."

"Yes. I know. We just have to get through tonight." Marcy clung to him, this wonderful man who had been working so hard for months to keep her and those she loved dearly safe. He was a protector; she thought of the belt buckle she had bought him from Gant Meadows. There would never be a way to repay him for all he had done for her these past few months. He had brought love and hope back into her life and kept her safe from an evil woman who destroyed her family and now wanted nothing more than to wipe them all from the face of the earth for money. "Blake," she whispered in the hollow of his neck. "I love you."

"I love you, too, Marcy. So very much."

CHAPTER 27

Blake was manning communications in Banderas when the call came in. Nancy and Corey had been spotted entering Boots. The decoy would follow them into the establishment in five minutes. Just enough time for Nancy to order a drink and begin to scheme.

Sheriff Riggs was by his side. Logan and Rodriguez were also listening over the radio to the operation. Amanda, too, was there as a consultant and observer. Blake owed her for the time she'd spent putting the plan into motion. She had gotten the decoy in place and had a makeup team on the way to Marcy's. They would hide their vehicle in the garage as would he in case Nancy decided to check herself, though he doubted she would. However, she might send in Corey to keep an eye on the biker.

"Gray Johnston is getting off his bike out front," called the deputy sitting in the back of unmarked van across the street. "We are a go."

The plan was in motion. Blake felt a frisson of high energy in the room. He hoped it went smoothly. Marcy was worn out from the stress and anxiety eating away at her. But Gray Johnston was good. He looked like a badass biker in every way. He was an undercover agent in Houston, had been working the streets for years, and went by the nickname Blue Balls in that area. To MC clubs in the state, he was an unpatched biker flitting from place to place trying to break into one of the local clubs. Amanda had great faith in his ability to be convincing. He was wired as well, so they all could listen to the conversation going on inside Boots.

The mic was taped securely to an area high up on his back and could not be detected through the leather vest he wore. A rough voice cut in. "I spot the suspects. They are sitting at the end of the bar. I will take a position nearby."

Blake was on pins and needles.

"Whiskey, straight up," Blue Balls ordered after the bartender asked what he was having to drink.

"Never seen you around," the bartender remarked, sliding a drink to the rough-looking customer. Gray's short black hair was in complete disarray with gray peppered throughout. It looked like he hadn't bathed in a month.

"Yeah, well, I'm a lone wolf looking for an MC to join. You got any good ones in the area that see action?" Gray asked the bartender.

"There's a few. I don't know about action, but a lot of bikers come in here, usually a little later in the evening. I can point them out to you, if you like."

Gray grunted in response. The quality of the mic was so good, Blake and the others could hear the man swallow his whiskey. "Another," he demanded of the bartender. "As I said, I'm looking for a club that sees some action. Not one of those pansy ones who just do it for the love of riding."

"We got those, true, but a few of the others have a reputation for being rule benders."

"That's good 'cuz I need cash fast," he said a little louder. "Got myself into some trouble in Houston and owe a few guys big time."

"Sorry to hear about your troubles. I'll point them out, like I said," the bartender replied, his voice fading as he moved down the bar to serve other customers.

Gray didn't have long to wait for Nancy to strike. Like the true predator she was, she pounced after overhearing his conversation with the bartender.

"Well, how are you doing, handsome?" Her voice sounded sultry, and it turned Gray's stomach.

"Just fine, sexy." The blonde was in a hurry, Gray thought. It made her desperate, and desperate people made mistakes. Another thing he noticed was her smile; her lips boosted with Botox were as plump as cherries, but the smile didn't reach her eyes. More botox or just cold-blooded.

"Funny name," Nancy noted, tracing her fingernail over the lettering on the back of his jacket. Then she came up beside him and continued to trail her finger over his shoulder and up his neck. She tried to entice him with sex. It was her lure, her bait, and she was trying to hook him. "Blue Balls?" she laughed. "Can I guess why you got that nickname?"

"It ain't rocket science, sexy. I got an old lady," he lied, "and when she is around well, let's just say I can't play. I can promise you everything works real fine downtown. And good news for you, my old lady ain't around right now."

Nancy took the seat next to him, thinking she had her hooks in deep, but the other suspect remained where he was, drinking alone. Gray kept one eye on him. Corey was observing, waiting to swoop in case there was trouble. Gray eyed the man watching the two of them in the mirror across the bar from under his heavy brows. Gray did not give himself away. He noticed everything.

She leaned forward and laughed, showing him her double plastic D's clearly visible in her buttoned-down blouse.

"You got a nice rack, baby. Want to get a room?" he suggested and noticed the man's face in the mirror cloud over. He didn't like his woman sleeping around, though she was known for it.

"Actually, I wanted to make you a different kind of offer." She arched one eyebrow up to entice him.

"I don't pay for it, lady." He intentionally miscon-strued her statement.

She laughed. "I'm not a professional, if that is what you are inferring. But, I'm also not a lady. My name is Danielle," Nancy lied, crooning the words seductively into his ear. She leaned closer, licked his cheek, and swirled her tongue in his ear until she pulled the lobe of it into her mouth, playfully biting it.

"Hmm, so what are you then?" Gray asked, pretending to enjoy her fake advances. He put his arm around her and grabbed her ass hard.

"Ooo, I do like it rough, but the offer I have for you doesn't involve sex, unless you want it. I am game."

"God, your ass is rock hard. I sure would love to give it a tap. Have you on your knees."

"That can be arranged. And thank you. Pilates and yoga every day. Hot yoga."

"I like the sound of that. So, what's the offer?"

Nancy paused long enough to make him sweat. "Well, I couldn't help but hear you need cash. I actually have a job, but I am wondering how far you're willing to go? What type of jobs would you do?"

Gray didn't want to jump the gun. He wanted her to think he was hard up. He sighed. "Frankly, I would do anything right about now. I need a lot of dough to pay some guys I owe. These guys don't like to wait." He made his voice hard and menacing. He wanted her to know he meant it. Then added, "What do you have in mind?"

"I have a real pain in the ass I need taken out. I could pay you really well."

"Taken out? You need me to beat the shit out of someone, teach them a lesson? Just what are we talking about?" She had to say the words. Gray had to get her to say it or else this conversation would stand for shit in court.

Nancy shook her head. She put her hand on Blue

Balls' cock and gave it a gentle squeeze and rub. She kept rubbing until Gray responded by growing hard. "'Fraid not. It's a woman and I need her dead. Are you man enough for that?"

This was where it got tricky. Gray needed her not only to ask him to do it, but she had to pay him. It could not be an in-the-moment thing. So he would not give in easily. "Dead, huh?" He made it look like he was waffling a bit. "I need another drink down here?" Gray called to the bartender. Nancy backed up a bit. The bartender came by and poured him another shot. "Leave the bottle." The bartender nodded when he saw the fifty Gray put on the counter and backed away.

When the bartender was out of earshot, Gray risked a look in Corey's direction and noticed he was paying more attention. "When do you need this job done? I'm not from around here and don't know how long I'm staying. The sooner the better. I got a debt to pay." Gray licked his lips to make himself look shifty.

"Five Gs should cover it," Nancy offered.

"Fuck no! Ten. And I need half up front."

"I don't carry that kind of cash with me. I can do two hundred now. The rest after, when I have proof." Her eyes shifted and Gray knew she was lying about how much money she carried with her.

"Fuck off, lady." He lowered his gruff voice. "You want me to off a broad, I gotta have more than that." He waved his hand to shoo her away. She didn't move.

"How about," Nancy mused, "my engagement ring. It's got to be worth at least 10k. You meet me at the corner of Lennox and Briarwood in the morning, nine

AM. There is a gas station there, and my bank is across the street. You come *with* proof and give me back the ring. I will have your cash then."

Gray narrowed his eyes, but made it seem like he was thinking. "What if you don't show and I'm stuck with the ring? I need cash, Danielle. I ain't got time to pawn it. Plus, it might be hot. I don't know who the hell you are." Gray poured a fourth drink he didn't plan to have. He had her on the ropes.

"Oh, I'll show up. My fiancée will blow a gasket if I lose the ring. Plus, I want proof the deed is done."

"I don't know. I could really use the cash. How much you got on you? And don't bullshit me."

Nancy made a face. She carried around a little mad money in an envelope in her checkbook. A thousand dollars. It was emergency money in case she wanted to get something she didn't want her father seeing on her credit card statements. That and a couple hundred in her wallet. "I can give you twelve hundred now."

Gray waited a moment before he stuck out his hand. "Deal."

Nancy smiled, pleased with herself, Gray thought. The woman was a narcissistic sociopath. She reached for her purse, pulled out two hundred-dollar bills from her wallet and fished the rest out of her envelope.

He looked inside. "And the ring?" Nancy nodded and slipped it off her finger.

Gray stood and dropped it into his pocket. "Photos

good?" he asked. She looked confused for a moment. "Of the victim, the woman you want dead."

"Oh, yes, that would be perfect."

"You want me to send them to you or show you in person?"

"In person would be best. I don't want anything like that on my phone. You know, just in case."

Oh, he knew. Nothing that could be traced to her. She didn't realize the entire thing was being recorded.

"I ain't no rat, lady. And I don't get caught."

"That's good to hear." Gray began to walk away. "One more thing." He paused and turned back around to the blonde. "Make it hurt a little first." Bitch was cold.

He gave her one more nod and walked out. His job was almost done and the so-called lady would pay for her crimes. Gray smiled. He liked an easy job.

* * *

Blake smiled triumphantly as Jack clapped him on the back. "You got her, New York. Damn good job. You go on out to Marcy now and take care of what you got to do there, but keep me in the loop. I've got somewhere to be tonight."

"Thanks, Jack."

Amanda spoke up. "Great job, Blake. You got her for the murder-for- hire without a doubt, and when you wrap this up tomorrow, you'll get her on the cold case, too, and the previous attempts on Marcy's and the boys' lives. She'll never see the light of day, and if you're lucky she gets the needle. Corey's days are numbered, too. He will spend the rest of his life in jail."

"Roger that." He was so damn glad that this was almost behind them. For Marcy's sake and the boy's, it needed to be.

CHAPTER 28

The makeup artist the San Antonio police department had sent to work on Marcy was an expert. Her name was Carrie, and she was super talented and patient. Marcy was a nervous wreck as it was. So she was happy that Carrie took the time to explain what she was doing as she did it.

Carrie started with a stippling brush to make Marcy's pallor more death-like and give her a mottled complexion. Then she began to apply some dark tones to signify bruises on her arms, face, and neck. Marcy shuddered at her appearance.

Gray Johnston, the biker who used the name Blue Balls was in the room. "Nancy told me to make it hurt. Sorry," he offered sheepishly.

"It's not your fault," Marcy said. She was glad Blake had let her call the kids earlier. She didn't want them to worry about her. She explained she had an allergic reaction to something she'd eaten, but the doctors had given her medicine and sent her home. She was resting and Blake would pick them up from school the next day as she would take another day off to rest. Plus, she could not go to school if she was supposed to be dead.

The boys had been relieved to hear it. They had been having a blast with Angel, helping him with the animals and feeding Abu, the camel he had rescued from a zoo.

The makeup artist applied some small prosthetic pieces that looked like dried glue. "I will paint these to look like scratches. The bigger one here will be a bullet wound."

"I really don't need to know." Marcy once again shuddered, and Blake reached for her hand and gave it a squeeze. Another artist was working on the clothes she would wear. They had ripped one of her favorite red flannel shirts, tearing off one of the sleeves. They also brought in a small bag of dirt and meticulously rubbed it into a pair of faded denims and the flannel to make it look like she struggled.

"Please grab a handful, Marcy, and rub it onto your arms and neck for me," the makeup artist ordered. Marcy did as she was told. "This will make it look like you tried to crawl away."

Rodriguez, who had come with Blake to oversee the operation, entered the house. Sweat dripped off his brow and Blake handed him an ice-cold bottle of water from the fridge. "I finished digging the hole in the back field."

Marcy nodded. Everything was in place.

Blake checked the app on her phone to make sure no one else was coming onto the property. Gray thought maybe Corey might have followed him to make sure the job was done.

"Okay, I think she is all set," Carrie announced and stood back to check her work. "What do you think?"

Marcy didn't want to look again, but did. It shocked her. She had a bullet wound to the temple, oozing fake blood. The bruises and scratches looked real. Her skin was a deathly mottled white.

"Marcy, honey, you ready?"

She nodded silently, tearing her eyes away from what could have been had Blake not been working on the cold case that led him to Nancy. Blake and Gray led the way, with Gray holding open the door for her. The others stayed inside. They didn't need to bear witness to her posing for her death scene. She didn't blame them. It was the stuff of nightmares.

It had grown dark, but a full moon provided enough light to get some decent photos that would satisfy Nancy and Corey.

When they got to the spot, Gray knelt in the dirt and crawled on all fours. He kicked at the area around the gravesite. The hole was about three feet deep, two feet wide and six feet long. A pile of dirt sat beside it to await her "purported" remains.

"What do I do now?" Marcy asked. She sounded like a frightened child.

Blake hated that she had to do this. He wanted to sweep her into his arms and carry her into her home and hold her, but he knew she could do this. "Let me get in first and I will help you down," he offered, jumping in. He held out his hands to Marcy and she took one step towards him. He lifted her up and let her body slide down his until she was touching the ground. He pulled whisps of hair out of her face and gave her quick kiss. "I promise a better kiss later. I just don't want mess up your makeup." His tone was teasing, but he was serious, too. Deadly serious.

"Such a gentlemen." Marcy tried to laugh but couldn't. She wanted to get it over with and afterward throw herself into a hot steaming shower.

"Okay, let's get this done," Blake said. He must have read her mind. "I'll get out and you lie down on your side, bullet wound to the temple showing like we told you earlier. Pull some hair, not too much, over your face. It's gotta look like he threw you in there, so one leg back and one bent."

When Blake was out of her grave, she lay in it. She did as she was told and left her eyes open, not blinking while Gray snapped several photos with his phone. "I got enough, man. You can get your girl out of there."

As soon as Gray finished speaking, Marcy scrambled to her feet. Blake was already there lifting her out of the hole.

Blake did as he had wanted to do moments ago. He swept her off her feet and carried her home.

"I'll fill up the hole. Take a few pictures and skedaddle."

"Thanks, Gray," Blake called over his shoulder. "See you in the morning."

* * *

The moment everyone left, Marcy had gone into the bathroom to shower and came back an hour later looking pale and drained. Blake could tell she had been crying, too. The night had taken its toll. He insisted she go right to bed, and he crawled in beside her and held her until she finally drifted off to a restless sleep. Only then did he rise to finish preparing for the next day and the arrest that was to come.

The next morning, Marcy looked much better from last night's ordeal, but he could tell she was still on edge. They both were. Blake wouldn't be happy until the exchange was made and Nancy and Corey were wearing a pair of metal bracelets bound for jail.

"Okay," Blake told her, keys in his hand. "It's almost over. I'm headed to town now, and within the next two hours, Nancy and Corey will be behind bars for a very long time. I promise."

She put their coffee cups into the sink and turned to him. "I want to go with you." Marcy picked up her purse from the back of a chair.

"You don't have to do that, darling. You went through the wringer last night. Why don't you stay home and rest? I can pick up the boys from school and see you later this afternoon."

She shook her head in the negative. Her face was determined and she stood tall. "No, Blake. I want to see this through. I have to. I can rest tomorrow. I need to see with my own eyes that they are in handcuffs. Please, I don't think I can sleep at night unless I see this for myself. Plus, I want to pick up the boys from school. Sign them out for the rest of the day. They may hear something during the day, and then there is Troy." She held up her hand when he was about to interrupt her. "I know he doesn't deserve it, but I would like to be there to help explain to him what was happening. He was fooled by her just as much as the rest of us, and worse, he actually loved the woman and was going to marry her. And goodness, she's pregnant with his child, possibly. I hope that was one of her lies. Troy has no real support in the area. He only stays in Banderas because of the boys, and well, because he met Nancy here. He is the boys' father, and I just can't stand the thought of him hearing this alone."

Each day this woman amazed him more and more. Her compassion for a man who did her wrong was a true testament to her character. God, he loved her! She possessed a toughness she probably didn't realize, and she was as loving and kind as any woman could be. He relented. "If you are sure, okay. I'll drive you in and we can pick up the boys after the arrest is made. Together we can tell them the truth. Then, we can go to Troy's, and I can distract the boys while you tell Troy if you need me to."

"Thank you for understanding, Blake. You truly are the best." She had finally found a man she could lean on and who would support her decisions. For that, she loved him even more.

* * *

Gray stood outside the gas station at the appointed time. He fiddled with his motorcycle to avoid drawing attention to himself while waiting for Nancy and Corey to exit the bank. They had gone in ten minutes earlier. He viewed their entrance at nine o'clock from the unmarked van across the street. Then he went to get his bike which he had parked around the corner. Now he waited for the final part of this operation to be concluded.

The deputy in charge of the whole thing and his girlfriend, one of the victims in the case, were hidden inside the van as well as the tech operator. Other members of the Banderas Sheriff's Department were stationed nearby in plain clothes, and some were in their unmarked vehicles in case the suspects tried to run. He wanted to help bring this woman down. He hated bottom feeders who preyed on the innocent for money. It's why he did this job. To put them behind bars. Nancy and Corey were scum of the earth in his opinion and far worse than the drug dealers and gang bangers he usually worked with while undercover. He was glad he could help out. At least they were upfront about it.

He glanced at the doors of the bank, looking for the perps. Nancy was dressed for the yoga studio, wearing a bright green neon tank top and leggings. Corey wore jeans and an expensive dress shirt. Nancy's BMW was parked in the lot beside the bank, and officers were close to it so they would not have a single avenue of escape left to them.

They were going down.

"There they go," said Mike Pearson, the officer who operated the undercover van they used for tapping and surveillance. He pointed at the screen, and Marcy watched the grainy images of Nancy and Corey on the closed-circuit screen as the couple departed the bank. Deputy Pearson had been able to tap into the bank's CCTV signal to watch the actions of the duo while in the bank. Nothing had gone amiss. The teller had not even batted an eye when Nancy asked to withdraw the ten thousand she planned to pay Blue Balls, the biker she believed had taken Marcy out.

"Okay, good. Gray, they are coming out. Let's get this show on the road," Blake ordered.

"Roger that," came the quick reply.

"Okay, Marcy," Blake told her, "we need to wait until after Gray shows her the pictures and the money has exchanged hands. The more evidence the better, and the less likely she will ever see the light of day."

And that's exactly what Marcy wanted. This monster of a woman was a threat to her and her children as long as she was free. Marcy didn't want her getting out of jail, ever, if it meant she could seek revenge on Marcy or her boys later. She had to get life in prison, heck, more than life for all she had put them through.

The tall blonde approached with her lackey in tow. It was clear to Gray which one of them was in charge. Pretty boy with the purposefully mussed up hair looked nothing like the woman. The fool who believed they could be relatives needed to get his eyes checked. But then again, Nancy had gone under the knife more times than he had fingers. The doctor had handed over his records this morning. He and Blake had looked them over and had known then the screws were tightening on the Barbie doll wannabe. The final nail was about to be driven into her coffin.

Gray grabbed his decoy cell and pulled it out. He had the pictures ready to show. "I think you will be happy to see this." He spoke gruffly and reached into his pocket for his pack of smokes. Nasty habit, but hey, everyone had to have one vice. He puffed on his cigarette while she flipped through the pictures Gray had taken. The smile on her face stretched until he thought her face would split. Corey, meanwhile, peered over her shoulder, his face turning ashen. He looked away.

"Yes, I am very happy." Nancy reached into her bag to grab the envelope with the ten grand in it. She held it firmly to her chest. "I have another proposition for you."

Gray's head popped up. "Give me the dough, lady. I thought this was a one and done deal." He took another deep drag, then blew it into the air, making smoke rings.

"It can be. If you say no."

"Give me the money first, then we can talk."

Nancy handed over the envelope and Gray was relieved the team didn't strike on the spot. He was curious to see where the fuck she was going with this now. Hell, she could put as many nails in her coffin as she liked. It still meant the same thing. A fucking eon in a dank, dark cell.

"Nancy, no." Corey tried to dissuade her from saying anything else.

"Shut up." She laughed nervously. "Nancy is my middle name," she told Gray, then jabbed Corey with her right elbow. "I hate it when he calls me that."

Gray looked inside the envelope. "More than I thought."

"Consider it a bonus. It looks like you hurt her, so I am pleased. But I have a couple of other problems I may want to deal with down the line. Not now. Too soon and all." She laughed again. "I was hoping to be able to reach you sometime."

Blake had heard enough, and at Marcy's gasp when she heard the words "a couple of other problems", he knew her mind went to the same conclusion everyone else's had. She planned on taking out the boys next. "GO. GO. GO."

Chaos ensued. Marcy had left the van to watch. She couldn't believe her eyes when Nancy tried to run. Corey had been brought down right away.

When Gray toppled Nancy, her face went into the pavement, and still the woman tried to fight him off, though her face was scratched and bleeding. Blake reached Nancy, just as Gray had her back on her feet, her hands behind her back with cuffs being put into place.

"You are under arrest for attempted murder, murder-for-hire, murder-for-hire with intent, false identity, theft, falsification of legal documents, and murder." Blake then read Nancy her rights as Logan was doing the same with Corey in the gas station parking lot.

At that point, Nancy spotted Marcy across the street.

"I didn't kill anybody. Look, she's right there."

"Yes, Nancy, you did, you hired someone to kill Marcy, and that is just as bad as murder. However, you most certainly did kill your previous husband, Cole Lansing."

The woman's mouth snapped shut. She knew they knew everything.

"Nancy!" screamed Corey. "Tell them I had nothing to do with it. Tell them!" he yelled as he was being pushed into the cruiser that awaited to escort him to jail.

"This is all your fault. You kept screwing up!" she screamed back as her transportation to jail pulled up next to them.

Blake began to steer her to the vehicle. "Gray, can you take care of this for me? Marcy and I have somewhere we need to go for a few hours. Make sure her call is to an attorney and not the doc. Marcy wants to break the news to him and the boys before it gets out."

"Got it." Gray pushed down on the blonde's head so she didn't bump it getting in with her handcuffs on, though he thought she most certainly deserved it.

CHAPTER 29

Marcy pulled the large Thanksgiving turkey out of the oven. The house smelled amazing. Blake had helped her cook a small feast to celebrate the day with her and a few close friends and family. Her sister and brother-in-law and their two daughters had come. Jemma and Angel were there as well. Jemma had made fresh pies, apple and pumpkin. Blake had been a great assistant and did well peeling potatoes and carrots, basting the turkey, and putting together the ingredients for his famous oyster stuffing.

She loved this kitchen and the open plan Angel had created when he put so much work into the house. Her table with the extra leaves was set by the boys earlier to accommodate all ten of the people who were already there. Jemma and Angel were outside entertaining the kids and the dogs. Her sister was making a quick salad to contribute and grilling Blake about his intentions toward her sister. It had been the first time she had met him, though she had heard plenty from Marcy.

Lena announced, "You are right, sissy, he is a keeper." She smiled at Marcy. She loved her sister and was so glad nothing had happened to her. Older by two years, Marcy was her closest friend. She couldn't have asked for a better sister.

Blake smiled. "I am glad you think so. But I think I lucked out, too. I know I have a lot to be thankful for." He gave Marcy a peck on the cheek as he carried the large bird over to the table. He was glad the feisty one, Lena, as Marcy called her, liked him. Marcy had told him how close she was with her younger sibling. He had liked her husband, too. Jimmy was a friendly and personable man for a corporate lawyer. Their two daughters, nine and eight, were sweet and polite and looked like their mom, with bright red hair and a scattering of freckles across the nose. He would like having Lena's family as his in-laws someday.

"Everything is ready to go for dinner," Marcy pronounced, wiping her hands on a dishtowel.

Jimmy, Lena's husband, offered to round up the kids. "I'm starving. Everything smells wonderful, Marcy. You have outdone yourself. I will get the kids."

"Thanks, Jimmy." She liked her brother-in-law who worked for a large corporation in San Antonio. Her sister adored him from the moment she had met him in college. Like Marcy, she had married her husband the summer after she received her diploma. Unlike Marcy, Lena did not work. Jimmy had wanted a family right away and provided the means for Lena to be a stay-at-home mother. She had never had to use her nursing degree.

Their folks had not been able to make it to Thanksgiving this year as they had booked a senior cruise awhile back. Marcy had yet to tell them about what happened to her. She hadn't wanted them to worry. But they would be joining the family for Christmas Day. After she and Blake opened their presents to each other, they would drive over and she would introduce Blake to her parents, though she planned to see them before the holidays to tell them what had occurred while they were gone on their cruise. Her dad usually did the honor of carving the turkey, and she would miss having them here.

With Jimmy outside gathering up the children, Jemma and Angel entered the house and took their places. "Bird looks great." Angel complimented the feast. "Who is carving?" he asked.

"Dad usually does it," Lena replied, "but I think Blake should do it this year."

"Are you sure?" Blake questioned. "You don't think Jimmy would want to?"

Lena laughed. "No. Jimmy is not quite as skilled as you in the kitchen. He orders some mean take-out, though." Everyone laughed.

No one spoke about what had happened just three days earlier with the kids around, but they all knew the truth. Marcy and Blake had called their friends and families and told them everything that had happened.

However, Lena was the first to bring it up that day. "I know what I am thankful for this year." She took her place at the table. "I am so thankful that you met a wonderful man who is truly worthy of the best sister in the world that anyone could ask for, one who is a partner, and in my opinion, a hero. I am so glad he discovered what he did, and those horrible people have been locked up."

Her sister's words brought tears to Marcy's eyes. "Thank you, Lena. I am too." Had Blake not pieced together the clues, she and the boys would probably not be sitting at the table.

"How is Troy doing?" Jemma asked.

"As well as can be expected. He…um… is thinking about moving to Austin. His folks are there and he said he wants a fresh start."

"Wow, really?" Jemma sounded surprised. "I guess you can't really blame him."

"It shocked me, too, at first. Before we signed the papers yesterday in front of the judge, he invited me out for coffee to tell me a few things. He amended the agreement. He gave me half the money from the sale of the house. He said I deserved it all along. I will be able to buy the ranch outright. He also told me he wanted to move back to Austin."

"I am sorry he is moving further away from the boys, but the other part is great news. What made him change his mind?"

"I think me just being there for him. He was devastated with the news at first about what Nancy had done. At least he found out she wasn't pregnant. He was so relieved about that. But he feels so foolish. He wants to be near his folks and some other friends from school. I think he needs it."

"She fooled almost everyone. He can't blame

himself." Angel was sympathetic toward the man. Troy had been through a lot even though he had done some pretty horrible things to Marcy the past year. But he was the boys' father.

Marcy shrugged her shoulders. "I guess. He hasn't told the boys he wants to move yet, so don't mention it in front of them."

"Of course," Angel and Jemma said in unison.

"Thankfully, he still plans on getting them every other weekend, and holidays. I told him I would meet him halfway between here and Austin."

Lena put her napkin on her lap. "You've always been so good to him."

"She's like that with everyone," Jemma declared, cleverly changing the subject. "It is why her students love her so much."

"It's why I love her, too," Blake added with a wink, while his comment received oohs and ahhs from those in the room.

"What did we miss?" Austin asked, eyeing the feast on the table like a starving man. His cousins, Elory and Amilee, his brother, and Uncle Jimmy were right on his heels.

"Blake telling us how much he loves your mother," Lena told him.

Her words didn't faze either of the boys. "Of course, he loves her, Aunt Lena. What's not to love? She's amazeballs. Now, come on, rub a dub, dub, thanks for the grub. Let's dig in. I'm starving," Adam caroled as he reached for the big bowl of mashed potatoes. "Who's slicing the turkey?"

"That would NOT be me," Jimmy stated with emphasis, taking the seat next to his wife, and there was more laughter. He looked confused. "What did I say?"

"Nothing." Lena patted his arm affectionately. "I already warned them to not let you near the carving knife."

"Oh!" Jimmy shrugged his shoulders sheepishly while everyone began to pass their plates around and reach for items on the table.

* * *

By the time her guests left, Marcy was exhausted and ready to call it a night. The boys had gone straight to bed when their cousins left. Blake, Jimmy, Angel, and Jemma had played a rousing game of football in the front yard with the four kids, while she and her sister caught up.

Her sister had just purchased a vacation home in Tennessee and had suggested she come next year for Christmas so the boys could see snow. She had invited Blake to come as well. Marcy loved the idea. And since Troy was spending this year with the boys for Christmas, it would be her turn next year. She accepted the offer.

Blake told her he liked the idea. He loved the mountains and to ski. They sat on the sofa together and sipped one final glass of wine before heading to bed. Marcy yawned.

"Tired?" he asked, taking her glass from her. He

knew she must be. She had worked so hard all day. The day before, too. After her court hearing in the morning, she had come home and attacked her house to make it shine before her guests arrived.

"Yes, I am," she sighed contentedly. "But not too tired." He saw the twinkle of mischief in her eyes.

"Well, that is an offer I can't refuse, Ms. Burbank." She had taken back her maiden name. He told her it didn't bother him if she wanted to keep her married name because of the boys. But she assured him it was what she wanted.

"I'm so glad." Marcy hooked her fingers into Blake's hand and led him to her room.

He laughed low in his chest. It had been a while since he and Marcy had made love. She had been such a nervous wreck the past few weeks, he had been content to hold her and let her fall asleep in his arms. He had been spending nearly every night there for the past month. He really needed to ask her if he could move in but didn't want to put pressure on her.

When her door closed behind them, he pulled her into his chest and claimed her lips with his own. He felt his desire for her immediately spring between them. God, how he wanted this woman in his life permanently. "I love you, Marcy," he whispered as he broke the kiss and began to push her back toward her bed. She began to unbutton her blouse and he followed suit. "I have an early morning," he said, as his shirt fell to the floor. "I've gotta swing by my apartment to change."

Marcy's blouse hit the floor. "You know, you should move in with me. I mean, you are here all the time."

A broad smile lit his face. "I was actually going to suggest it but did not want to pressure you."

"You know I love you. We have been together for three months, and I know it may seem soon to some, but you are it for me Blake Levine. I don't want to rush into marriage, but I definitely, want you to be a permanent part of my life."

He laughed as his pants joined his shirt and her skirt and shoes. "I mean, we have already planned next year's vacation, right?"

"Right." Marcy removed her bra and all thoughts of conversation disappeared as Blake scooped her into his arms and placed her on the center of the bed.

Blake's hand cupped and caressed one breast as he took her lips in a searing kiss that ignited the flames of desire within her. He kissed her until she lost her breath.

When Marcy's hand slid down between them and grasped his cock, he let out a groan of pleasure. They were both ready, but Blake didn't want to rush it. It wasn't every day the woman you loved asked you to move in with her. He took it slow, wanted her to remember this night, them together. He pulled her on top of him, knew she liked it better this way, and gave her the control. She leaned in for a kiss, and he felt her nipples press hard into his chest. Her full breasts were a sight to behold and just imagining them made his cock harden even more.

He stroked her back lightly as she began to move on top of him, sliding her core against his shaft so enticingly. She was getting into it and nearly ready. When she slid onto him, taking him all in so deep, he nearly exploded, but she needed more friction, so he held on, biting his bottom lip while she rode him hard. Her heat was wet, and he could feel her pussy clasp around him. From the sound of her moans, he knew she was close. He held onto one hip to help steady her and positioned his thumb at the apex of her entrance, gently scraping his thumb on her clit until she exploded, and he right after.

She lay across his torso, heaving with the intensity of her orgasm. "I love you," she whispered into his chest.

"I love you, too, babe. I love you, too."

EPILOGUE

Marcy curled up next to Blake on the rug in front of the fireplace. He had lit a fire, and they had just finished making love. It was nearly midnight on Christmas Eve. The twins were spending the holiday with their father in Austin. He had sold both of his properties locally and had bought a condo in a high-rise. The boys had called earlier to tell her how much fun they were having with their dad. She was happy for them. They would get to explore the city and see a different side of life from the one she provided for them on the ranch. They would get the best of both worlds and two parents who loved them unconditionally.

And now she had Blake. He had moved in three weeks earlier. Her life was full. The nightmares of the past were behind her. Blake excelled at work. He had solved two cold cases, and of course, worked as much as he could on his two new cases and with his volunteer work with the TVFD. The boys loved and respected him. There truly wasn't anything more she could ask for.

Blake lay on his side looking down at her. "Shall we open our gifts?" he teased, running his finger around one nipple. It quickly puckered under his touch, though she had barely recovered from their last bout of lovemaking.

"I thought we were going to wait until Christmas morning?"

"You are so beautiful, and I feel like the luckiest man alive. I want to give you my gift now."

Marcy felt lucky to have him. She relented. "Okay, but you have to open mine first." She sat up, pulling the blanket with her and reached for her gift to him. The belt buckle she had purchased from G-man.

Blake sat beside her, sharing the blanket. He opened the brightly wrapped gift and saw the buckle with the intricate design.

"It's a knot shield, an ancient Celtic symbol representing protection. Warriors would adorn their weapons and armor with it to keep them safe or ward off evil spirits. I thought it fit what you mean to me. What I went through was difficult, and I don't think I would have gotten through these past few months without you, Blake. I love you so much. I feel safe, loved, and protected. You make me feel cherished. I hope you like it."

Blake was overcome. It was how he felt when he was with her. He wanted to protect her from all the bad in the world. Keep her and the boys safe. He loved her and would always cherish her. "Here," he handed her the small box.

She tilted her head sideways at it. She must guess it was a ring. The size and shape gave it away. She pulled the wrapping off the small package and saw the black velvet box. "Blake?"

Instead of answering, he took the box from her. He turned it toward her and lifted the lid. He exposed the simple square-shaped diamond with the eternity loop scrolled into the gold band. "I know it's soon, Marcy. But I love you, woman. I am not going anywhere. You don't have to wear it or say yes, but I want you to have this. It was my mother's, and when I told her how I felt about you, she mailed it to me. It is yours. You are the woman I want to be with forever."

Tears sprang into Marcy's eyes. "Go ahead," she prompted him. "Ask me."

Blake smiled and took the ring out of the box. "Marcy, would you do me the greatest honor of my life and agree to someday becoming my wife?"

"Yes," she replied without hesitation. "I most certainly will."

Get the next book in Season 2 of the Tarpley VFD, *Fighting for Bree* available NOW!

Sneak Peek at Fighting for Bree

Years Before...

"For the last time, having a pen name will not make you a superhero," my younger sister, Calliope states. She's acting frustrated with me, but I see her smiling.

I hold up my hand, one finger at a time. "Bruce Wayne was Batman, Clark Kent was Superman, Peter Parker was Spiderman." I shake my head pretending disappointment that she doesn't agree with my reasoning, so I try to wrap it all up and bring it home. Again. "Lawrence Slater is a second persona to keep my true identity hidden. Ergo, I'm a superhero." Then I stand and, reminiscent of our favorite skit, execute the perfect Mary Katherine Gallagher stance and declare, "Superhero."

I also hope you check out the other five books in this spin off series Badge of Honor: Tarpley VFD Season 2.

Fighting for Amanda **By TL Reeve**
Fighting for Marcy **By MJ Nightingale**
Fighting for Bree By Haven Rose
Fighting for Lorna **By Deanndra Hall**
Fighting for Justice **by Silver James**

NOTE FROM THE AUTHOR

I hope you enjoyed Fighting for Marcy as much as I loved writing it. It was so much fun to create the Tarpley Volunteer Fire Department world that was hinted at in Susan Stoker's book Justice for Erin (Book 9 in the Badge of Honor Series). Her world and her fans are truly the best out there. So, I hope you have enjoyed each and every book in this spin-off series.

In season 2, I got to continue to work with the MOST amazing authors. Over two years of working together, we have bonded over the tough times that 2020 brought to each of our doors, and still we continued to support each other's work and plod on. These women, each one, means so much to me now. We also had a blast bouncing ideas off each other as we plotted out our crazy tales and how they would intersect this time around. The other authors in season 2 are the talented and uplifting Silver James, the fun and full of heart, Deanndra Hall, the sweet and accommodating Haven Rose, and the amazing and full of grace

TL Reeves. I could not have asked to work with a better group of ladies. They made working on this project fun and exciting as we weaved our stories into a cohesive whole.

Also, it was also pleasure writing for you guys, Susan Stoker's fans, who are truly some of the best fans out there. I am a huge, huge fan of Susan's, too, and I hope you think I did her world and her characters justice in this book. I hoped you like seeing Penelope, Conor, Erin and Short Shit again! I wanted to do her proud and did not want to disappoint you, her readers. If you enjoyed this book, I would love it so much if you could leave a review. It doesn't have to be long.

Please. Reviews help authors so much.

Tarpley VFD Series

Fighting for Jemma
Fighting for Marcy

SEAL of Protection Fan Fiction

Protecting Beauty
Protecting Secrets
Betting on Benny

Secrets & Seduction Series

Fire in His Eyes
Afraid to Love
Afraid to Hope

Mystic Nights Series

Chances
Triple Diamonds
Lucky Strike
Black Jack
Betting on Benny

The Bounty Hunters Series

Beautiful Bounty
Beautiful Chase
Beautiful Regret
Beautiful No More

Paranormal Dating Agency

In Dire Straights

MJ Nightingale has been a teacher for over nearly three decades. But reading has been a part of her life since she was a child. She has been an avid lover of romance novels, and they have always held a special place in her heart. When not working, or writing, or spending time with her children, she devours books all summer long, and any type of fiction, thrillers, crime, suspense, contemporary, and drama.

She is also is a USA Today Best Selling author, and the author of The Bounty Hunters: The Marino Brothers. She has also written the Secrets & Seduction series, and the Mystic Nights series. You can always expect a wild ride, an HEA, suspense, intrigue and super steamy scenes in an MJ Nightingale book. She has published fifteen novels, all contemporary or erotic romance with plenty of suspense.

She currently lives in Florida with her wonderful husband, two sons, and a dog named Champ. And, she loves to hear from her readers.

You can contact her on Facebook, twitter, and Instagram, or visit her website.

Facebook:

facebook.com/pages/MJ-Nightingale/185806224943537

You can follow her on Book Bub here: https://www.bookbub.com/authors/mj-nightingale

To reach her on twitter (@nightingale_mj)

Check out her Website: https://mjnightingaleblog.com/

Or sign up for her newsletter to get sneak peeks and more: https://mjnightingaleblog.com/contact

There are many more books in this fan fiction world than listed here, for an up-to-date list go to www.AcesPress.com

You can also visit our Amazon page at:
http://www.amazon.com/author/operationalpha

Tarina Deaton: Found in the Lost
Aspen Drake, Intense
KL Donn: Unraveling Love
Riley Edwards: Protecting Olivia
PJ Fiala: Defending Sophie
Nicole Flockton: Protecting Maria
Michele Gwynn: Rescuing Emma
Casey Hagen: Shielding Nebraska
Desiree Holt: Protecting Maddie
Kathy Ivan: Saving Sarah
Kris Jacen, Be With Me
Jesse Jacobson: Protecting Honor
Silver James: Rescue Moon
Becca Jameson: Saving Sofia
Kate Kinsley: Protecting Ava
Heather Long: Securing Arizona
Gennita Low: No Protection
Kirsten Lynn: Joining Forces for Jesse
Margaret Madigan: Bang for the Buck
Kimberly McGath: The Predecessor
Rachel McNeely: The SEAL's Surprise Baby
KD Michaels: Saving Laura
Lynn Michaels, Rescuing Kyle
Wren Michaels: The Fox & The Hound
Kat Mizera: Protecting Bobbi
Keira Montclair, Wolf and the Wild Scots
Mary B Moore: Force Protection
LeTeisha Newton: Protecting Butterfly
Angela Nicole: Protecting the Donna
MJ Nightingale: Protecting Beauty

Sarah O'Rourke: Saving Liberty
Victoria Paige: Reclaiming Izabel
Anne L. Parks: Mason
Debra Parmley: Protecting Pippa
Lainey Reese: Protecting New York
TL Reeve and Michele Ryan: Extracting Mateo
Elena M. Reyes: Keeping Ava
Angela Rush: Charlotte
Rose Smith: Saving Satin
Jenika Snow: Protecting Lily
Lynne St. James: SEAL's Spitfire
Dee Stewart: Conner
Harley Stone: Rescuing Mercy
Jen Talty: Burning Desire
Reina Torres, Rescuing Hi'ilani
Megan Vernon: Protecting Us

Police and Fire: Operation Alpha World
Freya Barker: Burning for Autumn
Julia Bright, Justice for Amber
KaLyn Cooper: Justice for Gwen
Aspen Drake: Sheltering Emma
Deanndra Hall: Shelter for Sharla
Barb Han: Kace
EM Hayes: Gambling for Ashleigh
CM Steele: Guarding Hope
Reina Torres: Justice for Sloane
Stacey Wilk: Stage Fright

Tarpley VFD Series

Silver James, Fighting for Elena
Deanndra Hall, Fighting for Carly
Haven Rose, Fighting for Calliope
MJ Nightingale, Fighting for Jemma
TL Reeve, Fighting for Brittney
Nicole Flockton, Fighting for Nadia

As you know, this book included at least one character from Susan Stoker's books. To check out more, see below.

SEAL Team Hawaii Series
Finding Elodie (Apr 2021)
Finding Lexie (Aug 2021)
Finding Kenna (Oct 2021)
Finding Monica (TBA)
Finding Carly (TBA)
Finding Ashlyn (TBA)

Delta Team Two Series
Shielding Gillian
Shielding Kinley
Shielding Aspen
Shielding Jayme
Shielding Riley
Shielding Devyn (May 2021)
Shielding Ember (Sept 2021)
Shielding Sierra (Jan 2022)

SEAL of Protection: Legacy Series
Securing Caite
Securing Brenae (novella)
Securing Sidney
Securing Piper
Securing Zoey
Securing Avery
Securing Kalee
Securing Jane (Feb 2021)

Delta Force Heroes Series

Rescuing Rayne (FREE!)
Rescuing Aimee (novella)
Rescuing Emily
Rescuing Harley
Marrying Emily (novella)
Rescuing Kassie
Rescuing Bryn
Rescuing Casey
Rescuing Sadie (novella)
Rescuing Wendy
Rescuing Mary
Rescuing Macie (Novella)

Badge of Honor: Texas Heroes Series

Justice for Mackenzie (FREE!)
Justice for Mickie
Justice for Corrie
Justice for Laine (novella)
Shelter for Elizabeth
Justice for Boone
Shelter for Adeline
Shelter for Sophie
Justice for Erin
Justice for Milena
Shelter for Blythe
Justice for Hope
Shelter for Quinn
Shelter for Koren
Shelter for Penelope

SEAL of Protection Series

Protecting Caroline (FREE!)
Protecting Alabama
Protecting Fiona
Marrying Caroline (novella)
Protecting Summer
Protecting Cheyenne
Protecting Jessyka
Protecting Julie (novella)
Protecting Melody
Protecting the Future
Protecting Kiera (novella)
Protecting Alabama's Kids (novella)
Protecting Dakota

New York Times, *USA Today* and *Wall Street Journal* Bestselling Author Susan Stoker has a heart as big as the state of Tennessee where she lives, but this all American girl has also spent the last fourteen years living in Missouri, California, Colorado, Indiana, and Texas. She's married to a retired Army man who now gets to follow *her* around the country.

www.stokeraces.com
www.AcesPress.com
susan@stokeraces.com

Made in the USA
Coppell, TX
08 August 2021

60156986R00154